Cariboo Lunewulf

Taming Heather

LORIE O'CLARE

ELLORA'S CAVE
ROMANTICA® PUBLISHING

What the critics are saying...

℘

5 stars *"Taming Heather* is a glimpse into another world. Ms. O'Clare skillfully weaves a tale of prejudice, change and love that will keep you turning the pages and wishing for the next book in the series." ~ *Just Erotic Romance Reviews*

5 stars "Ms. O'Clare is an extremely talented author that can ensnare her readers by creating characters that are incredibly realistic and erotically enthralling." ~ *ECataRomance Reviews*

4.5 stars "The romance between Heather and Marc is very hot, and the conflict between human and werewolf society is very believable, especially in the areas of the interspecies romance and the idea of werewolf children going to the same schools as human children." ~ *The Romance Studio.*

4.5 roses "A modern day rendition of the race wars of the past, *Taming Heather* brings to light all of the pain, betrayal, and love that only a story like this can bring out." ~ *A Romance Review*

4 cups *"Taming Heather* is a delightfully sensual romantic story, where Ms. O'Clare's focus is on the wild side of the werewolf. Marc and the other pack members embrace their animal nature, putting a unique spin on this wonderful story." ~ *A Coffee Time Romance.*

An Ellora's Cave Romantica Publication

www.ellorascave.com

Taming Heather

ISBN 9781419952951
ALL RIGHTS RESERVED.
Taming Heather Copyright © 2005 Lorie O'Clare
Edited by Sue-Ellen Gower.
Cover art by Syneca.

This book printed in the U.S.A by Jasmine–Jade Enterprises, LLC.

Electronic book Publication May 2005
Trade paperback Publication November 2005

Excerpt from *Pursuit* Copyright © Lorie O'Clare, 2005

Also by Lorie O'Clare

ဢ

About the Author

ൕ

All my life, I've wondered at how people fall into the routines of life. The paths we travel seemed to be well-trodden by society. We go to school, fall in love, find a line of work (and hope and pray it is one we like), have children and do our best to mold them into good people who will travel the same path. This is the path so commonly referred to as the "real world".

The characters in my books are destined to stray down a different path other than the one society suggests. Each story leads the reader into a world altered slightly from the one they know. For me, this is what good fiction is about, an opportunity to escape from the daily grind and wander down someone else's path.

Lorie O'Clare lives in Kansas with her three sons.

Lorie welcomes comments from readers. You can find her website and email address on her author bio page at www.ellorascave.com.

Tell Us What You Think

We appreciate hearing reader opinions about our books. You can email us at Comments@EllorasCave.com.

TAMING HEATHER
Cariboo Lunewulf

ഇ

Trademarks Acknowledgement

☙

The author acknowledges the trademarked status and trademark owners of the following wordmarks mentioned in this work of fiction:

Suburban: General Motors Corporation

Chapter One

This was unbelievable.

Heather Graham lay on the ground, her heart pounding against her bra. The ground rubbed hard against her elbows while she fought to hold her mini-camcorder still. There was nothing she could do about it.

Her eyes were glued to the small square screen, the red light glowing in the corner, the letters REC a minor distraction.

Add this footage to the recordings she'd already made, and she would have the story of a lifetime. Her career as a reporter would hit the roof. *USA Today*, the *New York Times*, they would all want her. *Heather Graham says it's so…* She liked the sound of that. Maybe that would be the name of her new column.

All she had to do was keep her wits about her, not do anything to fuck up this moment of a lifetime.

Lying in the woods, hidden by foliage, she hardly dared to breathe as she watched the scene in the clearing in front of her.

Creatures larger than any dog or wolf she'd ever seen or heard of moved around each other. A handful of them were half creature-half man, as if they hadn't changed all the way. The creatures she'd studied for so long now formed a small circle, passing around a gold chalice, sipping from it.

"We honor our dead in human and werewolf form." Their leader raised his arms to the full moon that glowed in the black sky.

Bodies changed and rippled before her eyes. Never had she seen anything like this. Or imagined it in her wildest dreams.

Unbelievable. Just fucking unbelievable.

Heather scanned her camera over the group of people. Some of them stood in human form, some had fur covering part of their bodies and others were almost completely changed into the beast that existed inside them.

There was no way not to react to seeing so many naked people. The glow of the moonlight outlined their sensual bodies, gleaming from sweat and stretched out to accentuate breasts on the women and the hard muscular chests of the men.

Of course the *lunewulf* would have to be fit in their human form. Running like they did every night in their beast form had to keep them in excellent shape.

She had studied these werewolves, allowed them to consume her life. Just a few years ago she was like the rest of the world, believing werewolves to be nothing more than myth. But now, with them popping up all over the world, coming out of the closet so to speak, she wanted to know everything about them. Her article would enlighten the world, clear the fiction from the truth.

Long shadows and moon casting scattered light added to the setting before her. The group in the clearing continued with their ritual. After more recited words they let their heads fall back, raising their voices to the night sky. In unison they howled, the sound almost like music as it consumed the night.

Heather could hardly control her breathing as her heart raced in her chest. Watching through the small lens, doing her best to capture all of the ceremony, she almost envied this extreme minority race. Their traditions, their culture, the strong bond they appeared to have with each other. Everything she'd studied showed how tight a community they were, existing peacefully for the most part alongside humans.

What baffled Heather more than anything was that humans had lived among werewolves for centuries and never even known it. If the facts were true, and she tended to believe them, werewolves had always walked this planet. Now bringing them even more to life would help humans see how peaceful a people they actually were.

Several werewolves dropped to all fours while she recorded the metamorphosis. It was the first time she'd ever watched a human transform before her eyes and suddenly turn into something so incredible, more ferocious than a wolf. The creature she captured on film had to stand almost as tall as she did. Shiny white fur sprang from their skin until it covered them. Muscles grew, contorting, bulging and shaping. Their heads changed, their noses extending and widening, darkening until they were black against the white fur that now covered them completely. It amazed her, watching their tailbones extend, grow and bulge until they were long tails.

It had to hurt. Her hands shook while holding her camera, but for the life of her she couldn't lose it and panic right now. Witnessing what quite possibly no human had seen before, she wouldn't allow her emotions to overcome her. They continued to change, drop to all fours, while she recorded the scene. Amazed at how these werewolves' bodies transformed, her mouth hung agape, her tongue so dry that it stuck to the roof of her mouth, but she wouldn't swallow. She barely dared to breathe.

Before her, not more than twenty feet away, stood more than a dozen werewolves. They pranced around each other, apparently delighted to be in this form. Regardless of how she could imagine the pain in a body changing like that, they seemed very thrilled to be in their monstrous shape.

The scene before her blurred when her hands shook. She tried to work the zoom, wanting a closer shot of them, but she was so nervous, her hands soaked with sweat, that she almost dropped her camera.

A twig snapped close to Heather's ear and she jumped, instinctively turning off the camcorder and shoving it into her jacket.

She barely had a chance to roll to her side when strong hands lifted her into the air.

Just as simply as that, lifted as if she weighed no more than a child. Landing hard on her feet, she stared up into intense blue eyes—that were raging with anger.

"What the fuck do you think you're doing?" Marc McAllister placed the human woman down on the ground.

Fear filled the air around him, but he didn't miss her aroused state. This human had been turned on watching them. He couldn't for the life of him figure out why some human would get her jollies watching werewolves during a funeral. Her fingers shook when she brushed a light red strand of hair behind her ear. But the defiant way she glared at him made him ache to teach her some manners.

The urge to send her sprawling through the woods had overcome him when he'd found her not only spying, but recording the private ritual. If she'd been werewolf he would have done exactly that. But her human scent surrounded her, weaker, fragile, less whole than a werewolf.

Already she'd zipped up her jacket, hiding her coveted evidence, proof of a lifestyle so foreign to anything humans had ever seen before.

"You have no right to talk to me like that." It was all she could do to speak, her mouth was so dry.

Something other than panic surged through her though. The man who glared at her, standing bare-ass naked, looked like he could dismember her with one arm tied behind his back. Muscles corded and twisted under well-weathered skin sprinkled with the perfect amount of hair. He was damn near the sexiest man she'd ever laid eyes on. And she must be about ready for the loony bin.

She backed away from him, almost stumbling. Never had she stood so close to a naked man outside during the middle of the night. Not to mention a naked man she didn't even know. Her heart beat hard against the hard plastic camcorder pressed against her breasts. Her nipples charged with an energy that sank deep between her legs. There was no way she could keep her gaze from lowering, from taking in all of the incredible man who stood in front of her.

"And you have no right to violate the sanctity of this ceremony." He fisted his hands at his sides, aware of her drooling over him, indifferent to the fact that she disrespected him and his kind with her actions. "Would you have me parade through one of your funerals?"

That wasn't what she'd been doing. She didn't parade through anything. Somehow snapping back at him, saying just that, seemed a rather foolish move. This man was a stranger, but she wasn't a stranger to men. He was furious, royally pissed off, reasoning with him right now wouldn't work.

Heather backed away from him. His cock stiffened briefly when he snapped at her. His nudity made it hard to concentrate on what he was saying.

"I'm leaving. No hard feelings." She turned and hurried away from the man.

Not man...werewolf. And an incredibly outraged werewolf at that.

Chapter Two

ℬ

Heather's heart pounded in her chest. Her mouth went dry when she stopped at the red light, right behind the werewolf she'd seen the night before.

This was so insane. And it had been pure coincidence seeing him today, learning that he was a cop.

"He's going to notice you following him," she muttered, accelerating slowly and praying he wouldn't focus on his rearview mirror and notice her.

By the time she'd reached the edge of town her palms were so sweaty they slid on the steering wheel. Something called her, made her move forward. She had to follow him, see what he would do.

When he pulled off the road and parked in a lot of an isolated park, she could hardly breathe. Circling around, her car seemed to be on autopilot when she came up on the park once again. His car sat in the darkness, appearing abandoned. He was nowhere around.

The cold Canadian night air wrapped around her. More than likely it was nerves that made her shake more than the cold though. After parking her car on the opposite side of the parking lot from his, and walking across the lot in the dark, she wasn't so sure how smart it had been to come out here alone.

She was in an isolated part of town. No one knew she was here. And she was tracking a werewolf—a very large, dangerous, deadly werewolf.

If I get out of here alive, I swear I will never do anything so crazy again.

Heather's heart wouldn't stop pounding. Her palms were so wet it wasn't even funny. But she couldn't run. She couldn't leave. Never in her life had she imagined she would be witnessing something like this. And it had her frozen where she stood, staring in disbelief and fascination.

You've got enough research on these werewolves, and you damn well know you are pushing your luck.

But there was no way Heather could back out now.

A trickle of sweat dripped down between her breasts. She ached to reach under her shirt and wipe it away, but there was no way she'd move.

He'd see her. And she wasn't sure what would happen if he did.

As terrified as she was, watching the beast saunter through the woods, move with more grace than she ever would have imagined a creature of that size doing, she didn't want to lose him. There was no logic to it. She was scared to death, yet more excited than she'd ever been in her life.

Her nipples hardened against her sweater, and the seam of her jeans rubbed against her pussy, which was already soaked. It made no sense that a beast, a creature, a deformed wolf, would turn her on so damned much. It was sick, worse than perverted. A creature shouldn't have her insides throbbing with more excitement than she'd ever experienced in her life.

But it couldn't be sexual arousal. Heather Graham was a normal woman. And animals didn't turn on normal women. An oversized, deformed wolf wasn't going to make her ache to drop to all fours and be fucked. No. That wasn't it at all. It was the excitement of finding him, of watching him move slowly through the woods, his muscles rippling under smooth fur with a cocky confidence.

Long fangs pressed against the fur under his mouth. Silver eyes were watchful of their surroundings. Shoulder blades glided up and down as he stepped without care, indifferent to the noise he made while he moved closer to where she stood at the edge of the parking lot, just at the edge of the woods outside Prince George. This creature owned the night.

Heather's breath tangled somewhere between her lungs and her throat when he came nearer. She could smell the earth on him, hear him breathing. As a werewolf, she could almost look him dead on in the face.

And then he turned, his large face staring directly at her. The moonlight caught a bit of his fur, making it shine. Never had she seen a creature like him. So white, so tall and powerful. It made her weak in the knees.

She didn't move. For the life of her, she couldn't. Branches snapped underneath him when he moved closer. Heather wouldn't dare think about the fact that he might have spotted her. An animal had stronger instincts. She should have thought of that. But in the excitement of following him, she had simply hurried into the night, still preoccupied after having been caught by him the night before. It still amazed her that she'd gotten away with her camcorder, and her sanity, intact.

If you were sane you'd be at home right now typing up the damn article, not out here gathering more research when you have more than enough.

The truth of the matter sank through her when he took that final step. His long tail swatted at the air behind him. And then his lips parted, his long red tongue moving slowly over dangerous-looking teeth.

Heather didn't know whether she was going to throw up or pass out. Either way she couldn't breathe, was too scared to make a sound. A low growl vibrated through him, rushing through her. Prickly chills rushed over her damp skin. The night air gave her a furious case of the shivers, and she fought to hold still. Her heart beat so hard it hurt.

And then he took a step closer. She was panting now, positive she was making enough noise with her nerve-racked breathing to wake the dead. Not to mention she shook so hard that she wasn't sure how much longer she could stand there, before she turned and darted to the safety of her car. A whimper escaped her lips. Her mouth was so dry that she couldn't cry out. Not that it would matter. No one would hear her way out here on the edge of town.

Damn fool. She was an idiot for following him this far out to the edge of town where they were so isolated.

She had a gun. The thought hit her and she fought to feel her fanny pack hanging around her waist. But her hands couldn't move to prove it was still there. She was paralyzed, standing there like a frightened child.

A cry escaped her when his nose pressed against her face, his breath hot against her skin. Sweat covered her body making her shirt cling to her. And she shouldn't be sweating. The night air was chilly enough, not to mention the temperature out here was probably close to freezing. It was as if she'd bathed with her clothes on.

He sniffed her. His hard nose moving to her neck. His dagger-like teeth brushed against her flesh.

Heather whimpered again, unable to control the tears that welled in her eyes. "Oh God," she whispered hoarsely, her throat constricting and her mouth way too dry to scream for help.

She'd wanted this so bad. Years of research had led her to this point. All the talk of werewolves living among them had made her mad with the need to learn all about them. No matter that they could kill, were incredibly dangerous, lived by a code so different from humans. She'd been drawn to them, determined to write the story of a lifetime, prove fact from fiction.

Why couldn't last night have been enough? She was a damn fool not to settle with the live recording of humans turning into werewolves and performing such a private ceremony. Hell no. She had to be superwoman and go out and gather even more proof. Except now she didn't even have her camcorder out. She simply stared eye to eye with a werewolf with no way of protecting herself.

The damn werewolf was probably learning a hell of a lot more about her at the moment than she was about him.

His mouth moved over her, his nose pressing between her breasts. Heather's heart had to be racing fast enough to cause damage. Every inch of her shook. There for a moment, she swore everything was going black. She would pass out, fall flat on her face, terrified. More than likely wake up with pneumonia from being out in the cold all night. Everything around her began spinning.

She fought it though, having to live through this moment, endure the horror of possible death. Everything she'd worked for had brought her to this moment, and she wouldn't let it go.

"Please don't hurt me," she whimpered, her voice cracking while she shook so hard she was positive her knees would give out underneath her.

The werewolf snorted, breathing in her scent as he sniffed her belly.

Heather managed to step backwards and instinctively grabbed her fanny pack where her cell phone and gun were. Those silver eyes gazed at her, showing more intelligence than any creature she'd ever laid eyes on before. They were almond-shaped, unblinking, watching with a wisdom she worried she couldn't compete with.

For some reason it hadn't crossed her mind that a werewolf might be more intelligent than she. That knowledge sent a wave of foolishness rushing through her. Why wouldn't they be? She was far from the smartest human on the planet. Hell, anyone with a lick of sense wouldn't be on the edge of the woods outside of town, too far from their car, and inches away from a creature capable of killing her with a single movement.

"I'm not going to hurt you," she whispered, her face burning with embarrassment as she realized how ridiculous she sounded.

Like she could hurt him. What she should have said, begged, pleaded, was for him to not hurt her.

His gaze left her. Either he understood and didn't care. Or he found her words completely preposterous. Maybe he couldn't understand her in his beast form. Something told her he could though. Even with her mind in a whirl of confusion and fear, she remembered werewolves had heightened senses in their beast form. More than likely, he knew what she was thinking better than she did.

His nose pressed against her again, continuing to explore her body slowly. And then he lowered his face, pressing his nose into her crotch just like a dog would.

But this was no dog. He was a werewolf, a man.

"No." She jumped backwards, this time losing her footing, stumbling, falling, before she could stop herself.

She sat on her ass, staring up at the ferocious-looking beast. Her entire backside stung from slapping the ground so hard. The werewolf lowered his head, large shoulder blades protruding above him like thick wings. He stepped closer as his mouth parted, long, shiny, pointed teeth glowing in the moonlight.

If Heather didn't know better she would swear he was laughing at her. Somehow that curbed her fear, strengthened her frustration and allowed her to think more clearly. This was an intelligent creature who'd just managed to knock her off her feet by copping a sniff of her pussy.

The nerve!

She had half a mind to jump to her feet and tell him just what she thought of him. But something was happening. He was almost on top of her and he was changing.

"Oh my God!" she managed to whisper.

Heather watched in awe, unable to fathom a thought, while muscles contorted under his shiny coat. The length of his nose shortened and his ears seemed to fade into his skin. The shape of his skull changed, while he began growing, straightening, his shoulders changing and moving backwards. His front paws grew longer while his back legs straightened and supported him while he moved to stand on two feet. Flesh appeared where white fur had been. Muscles rippled and smoothed, corded under flesh that now glistened in the night.

Standing over her was a naked man, his eyes the last to change shape and color as they went from silver to a radiant blue.

"What are you doing out here?" His voice was gentle, yet demanding. It seemed just a bit garbled as if his teeth still didn't quite fit his human mouth.

But his teeth were the last thing she was thinking about. She was sitting on her ass staring up at a naked man, and a damn good-looking naked man at that. If she straightened her head she was less than a foot away from a beautifully shaped cock. It took more than a little effort to focus on the upper half of this man hovering over her.

Blond and muscular with a light spread of chest hair, just the way she liked it, he looked like it didn't bother him in the least that he stood naked before her. She stole a glance at his cock, relaxed and uninhibited, his shaft straight and thick and surrounded by downy thick hair just a bit darker than the rest of the hair on his body.

Dear Lord. He was fucking beautiful.

"I...I was taking a walk." Heather blinked, hating how her voice sounded like a child caught doing something she shouldn't be doing.

"In the middle of the night? In the woods?" He grinned.

He was mocking her. And she didn't need to answer to him. They were on public property. The woods were part of the state park.

She diverted her gaze, unable to look at him and keep her sanity about her. It wasn't often in a gal's lifetime she had a gorgeous man hovering over her who was stark-naked—and a moment before had been a werewolf.

Heather's legs almost wouldn't hold her when she moved to stand. He grabbed her, stabilizing her jittery body with a solid grip that sent her insides into serious flip-flops.

"I think you were following me." He was all man now, his tone deep and sensual.

A chill rushed over her. She was way too aware of the strength in his hand as he held her arm.

"I was not," she babbled, unable to look at him.

Her heart still raced, but no longer from fear. Something else rushed through her, a nervous excitement she hesitated to label.

He pulled her toward him, and she fell into that rock-hard chest, feeling his chest hair tickle her skin. Heather's shirt clung to her from the damp sweat that covered her body. And even though he was the one who was naked, she felt suddenly very vulnerable and exposed when he took hold of her.

"Then maybe you wished to be the prey," he whispered, his arms capturing her, pinning her to him.

The strong steady beat of his heart pulsed through her, so unlike hers, which galloped to a furious beat. "And the excitement I smell on you is the thrill of being caught."

Dear Lord. He was seducing her. This was not what she'd expected. He was a werewolf, not even human. And she was a reporter, an investigator. All he meant to her was a serious boost in her career, the break that every reporter dreamed of. It made no sense at all that he made her mouth too dry to swallow and her breath come in gasps. Not to mention the fact that her pussy swelled, throbbing to match her heartbeat when he pulled her into his arms.

After the funeral ceremony last night, and getting a good view of him, Heather had found him the next day, kept a distant watch on him, until he'd taken off after work at the police station—how interesting that a werewolf was on their city's police force—and she'd followed him. It had all been in the name of the story.

"Let go of me." She struggled, although the struggle was also with her mind.

It had been a long time since a man had held her, or talked to her like this. Work was all Heather lived for, and this was uncharted territory. She didn't know how to react to the way he was making her feel.

Hell, how was he making her feel?

A wave of disappointment rushed through her when he did let go. And backed away—with her fanny pack in his hands.

Damned fucking fool!

He wasn't holding her. He hadn't been trying to seduce her.

He'd put his arms around her so that he could undo her fanny pack and take it from her. Anger took over.

"Give that back." She held out her hand, palm up, and glared at him.

There was no way she could take him on physically. Even when she stood as straight and tall as possible, five-foot two-inches had never been an impressive height.

And this man—werewolf—had to be at least six feet tall. Staring at him head-on, she got an eyeful of broad shoulders, and what had to be hard, well-sculpted muscles.

She sucked in a breath, willing herself to keep her thoughts straight. Right now was not the time to imagine how powerful this man might be. Although without any clothes on, he left little to the imagination. He looked a hell of a lot more than powerful. He was a fucking werewolf. Of course, he was strong. What she needed to be focused on right now was her article, how best to use this situation to help her in writing it.

He tossed her fanny pack away. It snapped against twigs when it fell to the ground, but in the dim light, she lost sight of it immediately. Her phone, her gun, her notes—everything was in there—her wallet.

"It's not going anywhere." He moved in on her again, those firm hands on her before she realized he had moved.

Strong and determined, he gripped her waist, pinning her so she couldn't move. His fingers were long, pressing against her flesh, which suddenly felt torturously hot.

"Do you make a habit of chasing werewolves?" he whispered, moving one hand to the center of her back. "First a funeral, and now a private run. Should I be flattered, or leery?"

She shook her head, a lump of nerves forming in her throat. He had her arms pinned between them. There was little she could do other than spread her fingers over his chest. Corded muscles moved against her palms, hard and pulsing with strength. His self-assured confidence soaked through her, reminding her that she dealt with so much more than a human man here.

"You have no plan of what to do now?" The amusement in his voice wasn't missed.

"I didn't think you would notice me."

"You haven't done your research then." His breath tortured her forehead, but she couldn't look up. "I smelled your scent before I undressed."

He knew she was tracking him before he'd started his run. And she'd thought she'd been so clever. And he was wrong, she had done all of her homework.

After recording the ceremony, she'd learned his name was Marc McAllister. Maybe it was a fluke that she'd discovered he was a cop while down at the police station earlier today. But she'd considered it a blessing.

And when he got off work he'd come here. The large parking lot, shaped in a U that surrounded the edge of the woods, had made it easy to stay out of his sight. She'd parked her car well out of sight of his, watched through binoculars while he'd stripped and then disappeared into the woods. And she knew she'd been quiet when she approached where he'd entered the woods. There had been no sight of him when she'd reached the spot where he'd disappeared amongst the trees. She'd sat and waited until he'd returned. And he had known all along that she'd followed him.

Damn hard to believe.

"And you waited for me," he added, moving his hand up her back to her chin and then raising her face to his with a finger.

Heather forgot to breathe, could hardly focus on what he was saying. Not only was he a werewolf, he was a damned good-looking man. Straight blond hair fell naturally around his face. Darker blond with a tint of red hair brushed over perfectly curved chest muscles. A small hairline scar next to his heart and another one on his flat abs added a sense of mystery to him, made him look even more dangerous.

She glanced up at his face, noting another, almost invisible scar along the edge of his mouth. Had he gotten all of these scars battling other werewolves under a full moon out in the wilderness somewhere? She met his gaze and dark blue eyes devoured her.

His grip tightened, pulling her against him, against his naked body. Yup, keeping her mind focused on what she needed to write her article was going to be one hell of a challenge.

"I was just fascinated by what you do." She felt like a babbling idiot. The right thing to do was to tell him she was a reporter. But somehow she had a feeling he wouldn't appreciate knowing he was being investigated.

"By what I do?" he asked, his hands moving up her back, his touch almost rough, and definitely determined. "Or what werewolves do?"

"Yes, well, both." Now she was definitely stammering like a stupid fool.

One hand gripped the back of her head, his fingers wrapping through her hair until he had a solid hold on her. He cupped her chin, pulling her hair just hard enough to heighten her senses. Her head fell back, her neck stretching while his fingers glided over her skin. She licked her lips nervously. He wouldn't hurt her. After all, Marc McAllister was a cop. He had a reputation to uphold. Surely he wouldn't want humans to think he was a manhandler. Not to mention, the Chief of Police was human. Heather knew that for a fact.

He held her head so she couldn't move, forcing her to look into the deepest pools of blue she'd ever seen. She could drown in his eyes.

"So are you interested only in how we celebrate death? Or do all of our rituals fascinate you?"

"Oh. I want to know everything." No matter that he had her head pinned. She blurted out the quickest answer that might help her learn more about his kind. And keep this conversation on a professional level.

Except she didn't feel too professional at the moment. If only his holding her head so that she couldn't move didn't raise her body temperature a few notches.

Damn. She was a reporter to the core. And at the moment, she wasn't sure he was in the mood for an interview.

Those blue eyes darkened, like a thunderhead ready to explode. She tensed, and his grip tightened. He held her hair tight enough that it almost hurt. Not quite, but enough that she should be getting pissed.

"Then maybe you'd like to know what we do with young bitches who traipse around after dark without an escort." There was a gravelly edge to his voice, enough to give the impression he was no longer amused.

"How dare you use profanity with me." She grabbed his wrist, knowing damn good and well she couldn't force him to let go of her. "If you're going to be rude then I'm leaving. Kindly let go of me now."

"If you were a werewolf bitch," he began, his voice noticeably deepening.

"Yes?" She managed not to flinch when his grip on her hair tightened to the point where her eyes almost watered. "What if I were a werewolf?"

He had stretched her neck, making her feel exposed, with her head tilted back so he could look easily at her face. Something in his gaze changed. If he weren't a stranger maybe she could read his expression better. But fear and excitement rushed through her, making it hard to keep her thoughts straight.

"Let's just say we take better care of our own," he grumbled. "Cute bitches out by themselves are assumed fair prey. If you were a werewolf, I would be forced to become your escort. Unless you're the kind of bitch who would rather run on the wild side."

His gaze dropped from her face, resting somewhere below her neck. Heather's breath caught in her throat. No one had ever accused her of having large breasts. And she'd dressed casually this evening, knowing she would be following a werewolf. Her loose-fitting sweater had to make it impossible for him to see how her nipples hardened into hard pebbles, brushing against the wool of her clothing.

No. He couldn't see how he physically aroused her. And she wouldn't give in to it either. He was being a pompous ass, and she wouldn't let him think he could imply what kind of woman she was, or call her names.

Nonetheless, she couldn't utter a word when his mouth crushed over hers, demanding, and hot as hell. He parted her lips with a swift flick of his tongue, entering her, devouring her, and she drowned in the sensations that rushed through her.

His hands moved, swiftly, like an expert at seduction, one sliding under her bulky sweater, while the other shifted on the back of her head. He tweaked her nipple, sending sparks of electricity dancing through her, out of control.

She groaned, and he let out a growl that burned her alive. Never had a man been so forward with her. His hand cupped her breast, his rough fingers torturing her nipple.

Everything inside her swelled. Her heart raced. Blood pumped through her, making her pussy throb with a need she hadn't felt in years. No one had ever turned her on so fast, made her ache to be fucked. And that was exactly what Marc McAllister was doing.

She turned her head, forcing him to quit kissing her. Gasping for breath, she couldn't let go of him, or force his hands off of her. He'd rendered her helpless with little more than a kiss. If this was how werewolves treated their women, then this was a species that were dangerous in more than one way.

"Little bitches who run alone are often looking for a quick fuck in the woods," he whispered, his breath scorching her skin. "Is that what you want, little one?"

"Take your hands off of me," she whispered, fighting for control in her voice, and hoping she sounded authoritative enough to impress him.

He did, and then turned without ceremony and walked over to where her fanny pack was. There was no way she could look away when he bent over, completely nude, and picked the bag up off the ground. His legs were long, evenly covered with the same downy hair that graced his chest. Dark blond hair with just a hint of red. Corded muscles rippled against his flesh when he bent over. And damn it, if he didn't have buns of steel.

In spite of the cool evening, Heather was way too hot in her jeans and sweater.

Her mouth went dry, then too wet when he turned around and she found herself staring at his cock again. Well, hell. She couldn't believe she stood out here on the edge of an empty parking lot with a naked man. And a damned sexy man, who was actually a werewolf, and who could suddenly decide to do her serious bodily harm.

But he wouldn't hurt her, would he?

The sudden thought of having sex with a werewolf made her skin flush furiously, wondering if he would be rougher, a bit on the wild side, more raw and carnal than a human man as he fucked her silly.

But this man, Marc McAllister, police officer and werewolf, had just insulted her, implied she was some kind of slut for being out after dark by herself. The last thing she'd do was give him the satisfaction of knowing that his nudity turned her on. She bit her lower lip, and looked away when he approached.

He didn't hand her fanny pack to her but instead held on to it and took her arm, guiding her toward his car, the only one visible in the parking lot. Something told her that he probably knew she'd parked her car on the outer edge of the lot, shaded from the dark shadows of the trees.

"A bitch is what we refer to our women as. It's not an insult among werewolves." He maintained his grip on her until they reached his car. "And we keep a close lookout for our single bitches, protect them. A single bitch running alone at night tends to gain a reputation. Until a bitch, or a woman, is mated, her family and friends keep a close eye on her. It's tradition and the way things should be."

"I'm not out running around. I'm working." She could still feel his fingers wrapped around her arm even after he let go of her. "And I know what you call your women, but I'm not one of them. I'm a grown woman, a human woman. I don't need my family taking care of me."

It was none of his damned business that she didn't have family in Prince George. Her job had brought her here, and she was almost always by herself. Obviously humans were different than werewolves in more sense than one. And the way she saw it, she was lucky she was human.

He let go of her when they reached his car, and opened his passenger door then pulled out a pair of jeans. God, she was salivating watching him dress. This was completely unprofessional. Obviously werewolves didn't mind being naked around each other. He sure didn't seem to care that she watched him.

He pulled his shirt over his head and then slowly strolled toward her, handing her fanny pack to her. "What is it that you're working on out here in an isolated parking lot in the middle of the night?"

Once again he took her arm, then took off with long strides that had her almost running to keep up with him. He walked her straight over to her car.

"Somehow I have a feeling you already know the answer to that." More than anything she wished she could calm down, get a grip on her senses, tell him she was a reporter and ask for an interview.

He was just so damned cocky though, and he'd gotten her dander up.

He opened her car door for her. "What I do know is that it's time for you to go home." He rested his hand on the top of her door, staring down at her with those deep blue eyes that about made it impossible to think straight.

For a moment she wanted to challenge him, inform him in so many words that she was a grown woman and would do whatever the hell she wished. Her look must have told him as much.

"You can go home escorted, or unescorted. The choice is yours."

"Well, I'm glad to see you think me capable of decisions now. I was beginning to think you're accustomed only to women who are doormats." Heather had been told more than once before that her quick tongue too often got her in trouble.

He moved around the car door, capturing her so that her only escape was to climb into her car. She held her ground though, standing there and glaring at him. So damned sexy, yet bossy as hell. Well, there was no such thing as a perfect man. Must be that werewolves were the same.

"If I thought you were a doormat, I wouldn't bother speaking to you, but would have just thrown you in your car." He raised his hand and for a moment she wondered if he would grab her hair again. Instead his fingers brushed her cheek, almost a gentle motion, so unlike how he'd treated her so far. "Or maybe I would've just thrown you over my shoulder and carried you back into the woods," he whispered, his tone turning sultry.

She didn't need to ask him what he meant by that. His expression changed, his gaze dropping to her mouth. Fire rushed through her so hard and fast she almost stumbled into her car seat.

It was on the tip of her tongue to tell him to follow her home. Something about what he'd just said, about women running alone at night gaining reputations, had her holding her tongue.

She got in her car, managed to start it without fumbling her keys, and drove away, his scent still wrapped around her.

Chapter Three

ഔ

None of it made any sense.

Marc ran his hand through his hair, knowing he would do well with a hot shower. Sweat clung to his skin under his uniform. And even though the air had remained chilly throughout the afternoon, and clouds hung low overhead, he was hot and irritable. It had been one fucking long day.

"So what's the deal?" The spokesperson for the group of teenagers in front of him made an effort to sound bored. "You going to let us go, or what?"

The two human teenagers among them looked at the ground, the salty smell of their nervousness hanging heavy in the air around them. The three teenage werewolves in the group scowled at him.

Times were changing way too fast. In his day, werewolves never ran with humans.

Marc sighed. The teenagers weren't who he'd expected to find when he'd responded to the call and hurried out of the station. And he was sure his fugitives were long gone by now.

"I'll let you go when your parents show up to get you." He gestured for them to start the hike back to where the police van was parked. "Now, march."

Reluctantly they began hiking through the dense trees.

"This sucks," one of the boys complained.

"Good luck waking my parents up." The spokesperson of the group gave him the once-over. "They sleep days." She curled her lip, hatred and defiance filling the air with its nasty stench.

They reached the van. He'd parked at the edge of the parking lot when he had been sure he could apprehend the humans who'd robbed the convenience store better on foot. The last thing he'd expected to find out here was this group, skipping school and smoking pot. Stumbling on them had ruined his chances of catching the men who'd managed to escape the human cop. He wasn't in the mood for rebellious kids.

"Get in," he growled, making the human kids jump, and the werewolf kids move slower.

Taking one last look at the trees he knew went on for miles, his gaze stopped at the opposite corner of the parking lot.

The night before he'd met the human woman there — Heather Graham — the strongly opinionated reporter for the *Prince George Tribune*. Suddenly he swore her scent wrapped around him, a mixture of lavender and desire. He pinched his nose, looking away from the spot where he'd held her in his arms.

Marc scowled, and slammed the van door closed.

Back at the station the smell of humans annoyed him. Usually working among humans didn't bother him. But something about last night had crawled under his skin. Heather Graham had been on his mind too much today, and he didn't like it. Her column was opinionated and whatever she'd been up to last night, he was sure it would bite him in the ass if he weren't careful.

"Call the school and their parents." He ushered the group of teenagers, every one of them now in a foul mood, into chairs surrounding the truancy officer's desk.

"McAllister!" the Chief called from his office, and Marc gave the teenagers a final scowl.

Max Milburn wasn't a bad man to work for, considering he was human. The Chief of Police was a fair and honest man. There had been some rocky ground when Marc first signed on several years ago, but the two of them had formed a respect for each other. Human or not, Milburn was a good cop.

"I know, you wanted two men and instead I bring you mouthy teenagers." Marc stopped at the entrance to the Chief's office. "I'll head back out and see if I can't pick up their trail."

Milburn stood from the other side of his desk. "We sent backup out there. I hope to hear word soon. Go talk to Beuerlein." The Chief lowered his voice, something he always did when he was about to mention werewolves. "Your pack leader has requested assistance. It's a matter concerning humans and werewolves. Beuerlein will fill you in."

"Rousseau called you?" Marc straightened in the doorway.

Johann Rousseau had been pack leader as long as Marc had lived there. He made it a point to make it to all of the pack meetings, knowing his job as a cop made him a useful tool for his pack. Rousseau was a good leader, and seldom sought him out unless matters were truly out of hand.

Milburn nodded. "Beuerlein just buzzed me. Go see what he needs."

Five minutes later Marc was in his car, headed to the other side of town. Once again, Heather Graham consumed his thoughts. Apparently the rambunctious reporter had cornered a few bitches and their cubs in the city park. She'd upset the women enough that one of them had called their pack leader on his cell. The situation had escalated, and now he was being called in for backup. Beuerlein, another werewolf on the force, had suggested he look into it.

"It crossed my mind to send out one of the human female cops," Beuerlein had said just minutes before while briefing him in his office.

"I'll go." Marc wasn't sure why he'd jumped on the opportunity.

It wasn't that he was thrilled about seeing Heather Graham again. Humans had never appealed to him. They were so fragile, not to mention their inability to change made them more shallow. Humans stuffed their emotions, instead of letting them out. For the most part he felt sorry for the species, half of a whole. No. He didn't readily agree to take the call because he wanted to see her again.

"I've already had an encounter with this human," he'd explained, although Beuerlein had seemed content to let him handle the call without explanation.

He parked the squad car on the edge of the park, somewhat surprised to see that a number of people stood where the playground equipment was. This little human bitch had attracted quite a crowd.

"So as leader of these werewolves, are you speaking on behalf of these women?" Heather was saying when he approached the group. "You would say that these werewolf children, these cubs, are safe to interact among human children even though they show a tendency toward fighting?"

"Just because our cubs got into a scrap doesn't mean she has to come over and stick a microphone in our face." The disgruntled bitch, who had a cub standing next to her and one in her arms, glared at Heather.

"You didn't stop them from fighting." Heather wasn't in baggy clothes today, but instead wore a close-fitting dress and heels. She had pale pink pantyhose on which matched the darker shade of her dress. Instead of her hair being pulled back like it had been last night, today strawberry-blonde locks fell in a stylish cut around her face.

If it weren't for the fact that she was human, Marc would say she looked damned sexy.

Johann Rousseau managed a pleasant expression, showing his true colors of being purebred *lunewulf*. He was always the friendly diplomat. "Now don't tell me that human children never fight."

Marc took that moment to enter into the group, patting Rousseau on the shoulder and then moving in on Heather. Something resembling embarrassment and arousal filled the air around her when she looked up at him. Green eyes charged with life took him on defiantly. Marc didn't miss the curious look Rousseau gave him and then the human reporter.

"Time to break the party up," Marc told the surrounding group of humans and werewolves. Immediately his pack members began moving away, their attention on their leader but honoring his request. "If our reporter here has more questions, she can contact our pack leader for an appointment."

He took Heather by the arm, wasting no time in pulling her away from the group of curious onlookers. Most of the werewolves around them were irritated, but amused curiosity floated toward him in the air. He knew what they were thinking.

The worst mix on this planet would be a Cariboo lunewulf and a human. And they were right.

"Where are you taking me?" She almost ran to keep up with his long pace, but he didn't care. "I'm not breaking any laws."

"Try 'disturbing the peace'." He kept a firm hold on her when she almost tripped in her heels while hurrying to match his stride.

"How about adding manhandling to that list," she added.

"You seem to like that manhandling charge." He looked down at her in time to see her scowl, although her cheeks flushed a beautiful peach color.

"My car is on the other side of the park." She rubbed her arm when he let go of it.

Marc opened the passenger side of his squad car. "I'll give you a lift."

She hesitated for a moment, but then climbed in, showing a fair amount of leg before running her hand over her dress to straighten it. He bet her legs were as smooth as silk with those hose on. He imagined ripping the hose from her body but then closed her door quickly, hiding the view of her legs. His cock stirred to life in his pants but he ignored it. There was no reason for fantasizing about this woman. She was human, and a pain in the ass.

"Why are you a cop and not pack leader?" she asked when he pulled out of the stall and headed to the parking lot on the other side of the park. "Your kind seem to have a lot of respect for you."

"They respect me because I am a cop," he told her. "And because I'm *Cariboo*."

"What's a *Cariboo*?" She turned in her seat, again allowing her dress to glide up her legs as she looked at him.

He only glanced at her briefly, needing to focus on his driving. The smell of her perfume wrapped around him, but she was aroused as well. The mixture of scents was rather appealing. Again his cock shifted in his pants. What would it be like to fuck a human?

He pulled into the other parking lot, spotting the car she'd been in the night before. "*Cariboo* are a particular breed of werewolf."

Stopping the squad car behind her car he looked at her again. "You'll show me any article you write about us before it goes to print. Is that clear?"

For a moment he thought she would argue with him. The flare of defiance made her eyes sparkle a magnificent emerald-green. She nibbled on her lower lip, and suddenly his pants seemed too tight. But instead of challenging him, she nodded, and then slipped out of the car. He watched her walk around the front of his car and get in her own before driving off.

A cold shower would be in order this evening.

Chapter Four

෬

It was harder than she thought, learning where a police officer lived in this town, especially a werewolf cop.

Heather frowned, reluctantly walking out of the station after the dispatcher on duty had refused to be of any help whatsoever.

"What do you need McAllister for?" The officer who stopped her had a badge on his uniform that said "Beuerlein". He was stocky, not fat, but muscular, with a blond crew cut.

"I have something I want to show him," she said, wondering if she was talking to a werewolf or not. There was no way to know for sure without asking, and she wouldn't do that. "Do you know where I could find him this evening?"

"A lot of the pack head down to Howley's before their evening run." So he was a werewolf, and she liked how he spoke so openly to her about pack routines. "Marc might be at home though."

"Would you tell me where he lives?" She smiled when he didn't answer right away. "You know it's not like I could do him bodily harm. I just want to show him what I'm working on. He asked to see it."

Officer Beuerlein pulled a cell phone from his belt and pushed a few buttons on it. He watched her with a nondescript expression while he held the phone to his ear. After muttering a few words that for the most part she didn't catch, he hung up the phone.

"Okay. You can go see him. His address is 2900 Wright Creek Road. It's out of town. Do you think you can find it in the dark?"

Heather nodded, already grinning. Granted, now Marc would know to expect her, but he hadn't turned her away. And she knew she would have gone nuts sitting at home alone thinking about him. Now she would get to see him.

It was a hell of a lot harder finding the small ranch-style home that sat well off the highway than Heather had thought it would be. Her heart raced in her chest when she stepped out of her car, pressing her folder that held her article to her chest. The cold night air whipped around her but she wasn't shivering from it. Unease and excitement rushed through her, making her knees feel weak.

Her excitement was because she was getting the chance to really sit down and talk to a werewolf, not because this particular werewolf turned her on. Just because the image of him naked, his powerful body and impressive cock, had taunted her all day, that wasn't why she shivered now.

The gravel drive led to a paved path that took her to his front door. Her palms were sweaty and she rubbed her hand against her jeans before tapping on the front door.

He filled the doorway when he opened it. The first thing she noticed was his damp hair, a clean smell surrounding him like he'd just showered. Then she quickly noticed his bare chest, and the way his sweats hung loosely around his hips.

Marc stepped out of the way to let her enter. He was barefoot too. Damn it. She didn't have enough defenses for the amount of sex appeal that radiated from him.

"I hear you want to show me something?" His suggestive tone gave her chills.

But then when he ran his hand down her back, guiding her into his living area, his touch burned through her. A flush raced through her that she blamed on the heat from a roaring fire burning in an oversized fireplace at the end of the room.

"You asked to see what I was writing." She took a minute to look around his place, noting immediately that Marc McAllister lived well for a cop.

A matching couch and overstuffed chairs surrounded a wooden, oblong coffee table. Hardwood floors had been varnished to a warm glow, and oil paintings of mountain scenes and rushing waterfalls hung on the walls. The glow of the fireplace and several lamps gave the room a cozy warmth with its dim lighting.

"And that is why you came over?" He guided her to the couch, his hand remaining on her until she sat.

He sat next to her, his gaze lowering to the manila file she still held clasped to her chest. His fingers brushed against her breasts when he took the file, and then set it on his coffee table. Her nipples hardened eagerly, and this time she wasn't wearing baggy clothes. She didn't need to look down to know the snug sweater she wore probably gave him a wonderful view of the curve of her breasts.

"Yes. I would love to hear your opinion on my take on werewolves." She'd rehearsed the line, and thought she sounded professional enough.

Although she was almost too warm, she pulled her leather jacket around her, needing something to do with her hands. Damn, he made her nervous.

Meeting the hunger in his gaze made her feel anything but professional. She let go of her jacket and ran her hands over her jeans, then looked away from him, nibbling at her lower lip as she looked around his living room once again.

Marc sat facing her on the couch and reached for a strand of her hair. If he pulled on her hair again tonight she would come right there on the spot. She just knew it. Sucking in a nervous breath, she fought to keep her thoughts at a professional level.

"And why is it that you are so impressed with werewolves?" he asked, rubbing her hair between his fingers, but not pulling.

She swallowed. "It's a human interest. There is so much about you that we don't know."

"And you think coming out here to my den this evening will help you learn more?" His voice had dropped to a husky whisper.

"I'd hoped so," she admitted, looking at him again.

His blue eyes had hints of silver through them, like bolts of lightning, charged with an energy that sparked her curiosity.

Hell, he sparked a lot more than her curiosity. His hand moved to her cheek, long fingers cupping her chin and guiding her face closer to his. She was actually surprised at how soft his lips were when he brushed them over hers.

Heather sucked in a breath, the smell of him filling her senses.

"What is it that you think I can teach you?" he whispered, his gaze hooded as he bit slightly on her lower lip.

Heather jumped to her feet, almost stumbling over his coffee table as she moved away from him.

"Well you could...you could tell me what it's like to change into a beast," she stammered, her fingers brushing over her lip that he'd just nibbled.

"It's the completion of all energy." He stood as well, moving toward her, like a predator would his prey. "The change allows a werewolf to release their emotions. We pity you that you aren't complete."

Heather turned on a dime. "You pity us? We don't turn into monsters."

"And that's what you think I am, a monster?" He gripped her shoulders and then slid his hand under her jacket, sliding it down her arms. "Why would you wish to consort with a monster?"

He took her jacket from her and walked over to a closet by his front door, then hung it on a hanger. Muscles glided under the flesh on his back when he moved. He had a perfect ass that his loose-fitting sweats couldn't hide. There wasn't a damn thing monstrous about him.

Heather ran her fingers through her hair, turning her attention to the fire that crackled with life in the fireplace. Images of the creature she'd watched the other night came to mind. She'd watched him change, seen the transformation with her own eyes.

Marc McAllister was a monster, a werewolf, or he had that in him. The sexy man seducing her right now was only part of who he was. She had to remind herself of that.

The reason she was here was to get his insight on her work. If she could publish her article and say it had werewolf approval, the attention she'd get would be threefold. It would boost her career to an extent she was sure she couldn't imagine. That had to be the focus of her thoughts, not this sexy werewolf-man who was way too smooth of a talker.

"That is the impression humans have of werewolves." She turned quickly to make her point.

When had he moved right behind her? She almost lost herself in those deep blue eyes. The silver streaks had left, and an intense blue, bluer than a rich summer sky, captivated her. She blinked to clear her thoughts.

"And an impression you might be able to help me with." She tried to move around him, to point at her article on his coffee table.

Marc ran his fingers up her arm, sending chills rushing through her. Her nipples hardened again. He was too much man, too big, too powerful, too aggressive.

"So you're here to discover what my true nature is, to find out if I am a monster or not?" He moved quickly, wrapping his fingers through her hair, pulling her head back so that he had her pinned. "And what actions will convince you, my little bitch?"

"Don't call me that," she whispered, her breath coming so hard that she suddenly was dizzy.

His other hand snaked around her neck, capturing her face, her head, pinning her so that she was forced to stare up at him.

"Our women are bitches, mated or unclaimed. Would you have me pretend I'm not a werewolf when I'm around you?" His mouth barely moved, the words whispered, caressing her senses with their meaning.

"For us, it's a derogatory word." She knew her heartbeat pounded against his thumb, which pressed gently into her jugular vein. "But I don't want you to pretend you're something you're not."

"Good." He raised her head slightly, stretching her neck, and kissed her again.

This time the kiss was deeper, his tongue parting her lips and entering her. Heather let out a small cry, more like a gasp as she allowed the kiss, her insides filling with a sense of need she usually kept well-suppressed.

He held her head tightly in place, making love to her mouth. There was little else to do with her hands other than to spread her fingers over his massive chest. Warm muscles quivered against her touch. His tongue impaled her, blinding her with a greedy lust, while she ran her hands over his rock-hard body.

There was so much of him. And even though she knew in her mind that he could be even more than what appeared before her, he was more man than most she had ever met.

He bent over her. Even though he'd stretched her upwards toward him, he was still so much taller than she that he had to meet her halfway. Her entire world had suddenly become Marc McAllister. Powerful, dominating, aggressive, and so incredibly dangerous. She'd be in way over her head in seconds if she didn't slow this down drastically.

When she tried to turn her head to end the kiss, his fingers tightened for a second, as if unwilling to let her go. But then he relaxed his hands, allowing her to break off the kiss.

Heather stumbled backwards, gasping for breath, her lips tingling and wet from his mouth.

"All I want is your help on the article." It was a desperate cry, her feeble attempt to regain control of her senses.

Her pussy throbbed, her breasts were swollen and aching for attention. Like hell it was all that she wanted.

"Don't lie to me, sweet bitch." His voice was thick, deeper, almost a growl.

She stared up at him. His blond hair stood slightly on end, and the silver streaks raced through his blue eyes again. God. She'd swear he was even taller and bigger than he'd been when she first walked into his home.

"What makes you think I'm lying?"

"I can smell your arousal." His words stole her breath from her body. "It's more than your nipples pressing against your sweater, aching for me to suck them. And I don't have to touch you to know that your pussy is soaked. It's not how your breathing is so hard that someone might think you raced around the block just now. No. I don't need to see or touch you to know how desperately you want me right now. Your scent speaks volumes, sweetheart."

For a moment all she could do was stare at him. His cock pressed against his sweatpants, while images of seeing him naked the other night in the woods filled her mind.

It dawned on her that his chest hair seemed to be thicker, that his hair was tousled on his head, yet she hadn't run her hands through it. He seemed taller, his muscles larger. She couldn't smell him, but she knew he was aroused also.

And obviously when a werewolf was turned on, they got more than just a hard cock. His entire body had changed. What if he changed into a werewolf while he was fucking her?

The thought scared the shit out of her.

"You're a good-looking man, but..." She wouldn't say, *but you're a werewolf,* although the words about escaped her.

Something hardened in Marc's expression. "Yes?" he asked, crossing powerful arms over his chest.

She sucked in her breath, licking her lips that suddenly seemed too dry. "I'm here to discuss business. That's all."

There was no way she could break away from his gaze while he seemed to stare right through her, see the truth even though she dared not speak it. Marc was not only a werewolf with heightened senses, but he was a cop.

When he lunged forward, she jumped.

Marc took her arm, escorting her none too gently toward the door. He almost ripped open his closet door, grabbing her coat and tossing it at her.

"The next time you enter my den, you will admit to your emotions. I will not tolerate a second lie." And with that he pulled open his front door, and almost shoved her into the cold night air.

Chapter Five

‮ജ‬

Marc took slow, long, deep breaths once he shut his front door. He knew he had a mean temper. It was a *Cariboo* trait. For the most part with his work, and interacting with the *lunewulf* in his pack, he'd managed to keep his strong emotions in check. Werewolves in this part of British Columbia were different than the *Cariboo lunewulf* he'd grown up with. Hell, his father had thrown his mother over his shoulder, taking her physically from her den when he'd decided she would be his mate.

Now he knew that wasn't proper behavior, and wouldn't be surprised if his parents had exaggerated the story a bit over the years while they repeatedly shared it with him and his brothers. But his upbringing hadn't shielded emotions. When someone felt something, they expressed it. Sometimes he could barely stomach the way humans stuffed their feelings.

He took another soothing breath, aching to tear open his front door and go after that little human. She was all wrong for him anyway. He'd told himself that numerous times before she'd shown up. It was the appeal of someone different, someone who ached to learn, for him to teach her. There was a strong appeal in that. Not to mention she was just about the sexiest thing he'd ever laid eyes on. So fragile, yet with a strong, daring personality. He liked that.

She'd worn jeans that had hugged her petite figure, and a sweater that showed off breasts that he knew had to be well more than a handful. And her scent, her sweet, rich scent when he'd brought out the passion in her. Heather smelled better bathed in lust than any werewolf woman he'd ever been with.

"Damn it to fucking hell," he growled, turning from the door and smashing his palm against the wall. His pictures shook against the wall, and the flames in the fireplace seemed to dance with retaliation.

Maybe a run would help soothe the fire that danced with even more fury inside him. It wasn't right that Heather Graham had stirred emotions like that in him. He ran his hands over his hair, messing it up even further than it already was.

Toby Beuerlein had called when Heather had asked how to find Marc, down at the station. Marc had given him permission to send her out here. Beuerlein knew she'd been here. The werewolf more than likely had a clue who Heather Graham was, that she wasn't mated, and he'd have to be blind to not notice how pretty she was. Marc trod on thin ice if anyone learned how he'd thrown her out. His pack wouldn't question him, but if she made a fuss among her humans, things could get sticky. After all, he worked for humans.

Now he definitely needed that run. It would be a cold day in hell before he changed his ways for any human.

He padded out to his back patio, his floodlight attached to the back of his house spreading light over part of his backyard. The land out here was beautiful, rolling hills and more trees than a man could ever count. It was incredible timber country. And he knew more than a handful of his pack earned decent money working in the yards.

When he'd first moved east to Prince George with his brothers to join this pack, one of the *Cariboo lunewulf*, Rock Toubec, had set him up with this home, selling a bit of his land to him. His brothers, Stone and Gabe, still lived in the small cottage they'd built together on the land. But after a year of living with his rambunctious younger brothers, Marc had needed his space. They'd built this house, agreeing they would help each other build a third house soon so they would all have dens and be able to bring a mate home. So far, though, none of them had mated.

There weren't many bitches in the area strong enough to take on a *Cariboo*.

Was Heather strong enough?

He growled at his insane thinking and walked barefoot out to the edge of his patio. Cold night air slapped at his bare chest, sending chills rushing through him. His human flesh was a weak protection from the elements.

Heather didn't understand. Her opinion of werewolves needed serious adjusting. She had called him a monster, implied that his kind wasn't good enough for her, that she found him repulsive, terrifying. He wasn't sure what labels she would use among her own kind to describe him, but her hesitation, the way she'd pulled away from him, made his blood boil once again.

This time he didn't stop the heat that surged through him. Stretching, looking up at the incredible star-filled sky, he embraced the cold night air, allowing the change to ripple through him.

His bones had barely stretched, his muscles barely had begun growing, distorting, altering their shape, when his heightened senses picked up her scent.

At first he thought it his imagination. Heather was so wrapped through him, his mind so full of her, that he shouldn't be surprised that her sweet scent invaded him, teasing him while he slowly morphed into his werewolf form.

The darkness around him changed to a light shade of gray as his eyes altered. Fur poked through his skin, covering his body, warming him instantly against the cold. He slipped out of his sweats while he could still use his hands, tossing them with little thought onto one of his patio chairs.

Muscles bulged through his back, down his legs, over his arms. The intoxicating pain of the change made him want to howl, take off in a quick sprint before he'd completely transformed. Nothing made him more complete, more whole, than the transformation into the carnal half of who he was.

Heather's unique smell grew stronger as the change consumed him. Turning, his werewolf eyes making it easier to see in the darkness, he paused when he saw her hugging the side of his house, watching him.

A flash quickly blinded him and then disappeared, and he realized she'd just taken his picture.

Well, my little bitch, you won't capture on film what you imply you despise.

He leapt toward her, and she screamed. It wasn't the first time he gloried in the fact that he lived outside of town. No one would hear her cries unless another werewolf was in the area. And in their fur, different codes of laws were followed. This unmated bitch was on his land, in his den. She was his to deal with. And right now she was about to learn a valuable lesson.

"Oh God." She howled again and turned to dash around toward the front of his yard. "Please. Please don't hurt me."

He fought the change, something he hated doing. But he would allow her just one moment to hear his words.

"Learn now, precious bitch. I will never allow any pain to ever touch you." His voice had altered, his mouth barely capable of speech in his half-changed body.

She stopped moving and simply stared at him. He hated how fear covered up her beautiful scent. Taking the camera out of her hands, he hurled it as far as he could. She didn't fight him, didn't look after the camera, but simply stared at him, dumbfounded.

He wanted to scream at how his appearance so obviously terrified her. Unable to hold out another moment, he quit fighting the change, which was worse than holding your breath under water for way too long. He no longer controlled the natural release that soared through him.

Falling to all fours, his body completed the transformation, allowing his natural pure state of *Cariboo lunewulf* to take over.

"Do you understand me?" she asked, her fear still filling the air around them, but her curiosity coming forth.

He fought back a toothy grin, knowing that would probably scare her. Instead he moved closer, nudging her face with his. He ran his tongue over her cheek, tasting her. Everything inside him hardened when her sweetness once again filled the air. He had to be very careful, fight the natural instinct that worked to be free inside him. Heather wouldn't understand how instincts took over with werewolves.

She took a small step backwards, immediately wiping her face with her hand. But she smiled, an absolutely adorable smile.

"I'm sorry that I called you a monster," she said quietly.

Her hands were shaking but the fear around her slowly subsided, its thick, pungent odor dissipating.

Again he moved into her, brushing his large head against her breasts, feeling how soft and full they were. She stepped away from him again, wrapping her jacket around her, covering her frail human body from the cold night.

"Okay. I can take a hint. I'll go."

The last thing he wanted was for her to leave. But it was probably a damn good idea. The longer he stood in front of her the harder the urge to fuck her surged through him.

"And...and you don't look like a monster." She still sounded a bit too nervous. "Your white coat is very pretty under the moonlight."

Pretty? He'd show her pretty.

She took another step backwards and he lowered his head, following her slowly. Heather half-turned to walk to her car, and managed at the same time to walk backwards, keeping an eye on him.

It would take no effort to stop her, change back into his human form, fuck her right here in his front yard. At the moment that sounded damn appealing.

She got into her car, started it, and then almost popped her clutch trying to drive off.

Damn it. There went his chance to run off his pent-up frustration. There was no way he could let her drive back into town in her current condition. Her nerves were frazzled, and although Heather needed to see that she'd bitten off more than she could chew, he accepted full responsibility in ensuring she got home safely.

He waited until she'd driven out of his driveway, then returned to the back of his house. The change reluctantly soared through him and he grabbed his sweatpants, then went inside to grab a shirt and shoes. He would follow her home, then return for his much-needed run. More than likely, that would be followed by another cold shower.

Something told him knowing Heather Graham would result in too many cold showers.

* * * * *

Heather was still shaky when she entered her apartment thirty minutes later. Kicking off her shoes at the door, she padded through her dark living room, thinking a shower might soothe her nerves.

There was no reason for her to be so jittery. Twice now she'd seen werewolves changing, transforming before her eyes. Hell, she had it on tape. First with the funeral ceremony, and then later when she'd followed Marc. Neither of those times had put the fear of God into her like tonight.

That's because you're letting it get personal.

And that was the biggest mistake a reporter could make. Right now in her life, there was no room for mistakes. Ever since she'd left Dawson Creek, moved to go to college and then gotten her journalism degree, she lived every day making sure she didn't do anything wrong. Nothing would jeopardize her career. She was on her way to the top, and this article would be her shoe-in.

To many, Prince George might not be a huge city, but to Heather, she'd landed quite the job writing for the *Tribune*. There wasn't a better newspaper in all of British Columbia. And with any luck, this article would capture national attention.

So far she'd managed to keep life in order, avoiding any chaos or drama that might clog her brain and make her lose focus on what really mattered. Of course that had meant no social life, no dating, nothing that would distract her. And up until now she'd been content—no, more than content. She'd been happy, damn it.

Maybe some of her nights had been a bit lonely, but she was working to better herself, become a known reporter. That might have meant keeping herself from getting attached to anyone, but it had to be that way so she could think straight.

After flipping on her bedroom light, and then closing her blinds, she slipped out of her clothes so she could shower. She stopped in front of her laptop, which was on the small desk that she'd brought with her from home, and tapped the mouse so her monitor would come on.

The article that she had printed for Marc to see appeared on her screen. It wasn't done yet, there were still some areas she needed to tighten, paragraphs where she felt more emotion was needed. She sat down in her chair, staring at the words on her screen.

Their bodies twitch and contort. Muscles and bones shift and change, allowing these people to transform into wild animals known as werewolves.

Marc McAllister in his werewolf form appeared in Heather's mind. As a beast, he stood eye to eye with her, his head huge with long, terrifying teeth. His body was thick, rippling with muscles. But his white coat, so shiny, glowed like a clear full moon on a cloudless night.

Thinking of him made her words seem rather flat, lacking emotion. Marc was everything emotional. He was so...so alive!

What was it that he'd said to her? *It's the completion of all energy. The change allows a werewolf to release their emotions. We pity you that you aren't complete.*

Heather had always fought to keep her emotions in check. Ever since her mother had died when she was eleven, she'd done her best never to cry, never to get too excited about anything, never to be out of control. Control kept her life neat and organized.

And now she was trying to write an article about a species that changed into a beast so that they could release the emotions they kept in check as humans. What a life that would be.

Heather sighed. Marc pitied humans. She didn't want his damn pity. Her hand strolled down her naked body, and she began stroking the ache between her legs while she pictured Marc in her mind.

The way he'd moved in on her, pressed his head against her body. Even before he'd made the complete transformation and had been half man-half creature, she'd been mesmerized by what he was capable of doing. His appearance had captivated her, scared her and excited her all at the same time. Just a few years ago no one ever would have been able to make her believe that such creatures walked among them.

Cream coated her fingers and she dipped into the source of her heat, surprised at how wet she was. She'd seen good-looking men before, but damn, none of them had turned her on the way Marc had. Granted none of them ever came on to her the way he had. Adjusting herself on her chair, she moved her fingers slowly in and out of her tight heat, wondering what it would be like if Marc were to do this to her.

Her head fell back and she lifted one of her legs, propping her foot on her desk next to her laptop. She ran one hand over a swollen breast, squeezing it gently while she continued to masturbate.

The ache to have her breasts fondled, tugged on slightly, made her want to cry out. More than anything she needed her nipples sucked on. Need surged through her like a wildfire.

Marc wouldn't do it this way, she decided. He would be rough, more demanding, pushing her quickly as far as she could go, and then demanding she go even further. He would be able to break through the protective wall that she kept around herself, force her to feel more than she'd ever felt in her life.

Did she want her tidy life disturbed like that?

She added a second finger, stretching her narrow hole and feeling the pressure build slowly inside her. Her fingernails brushed over her nipple. The sensation sent waves of need plummeting through her. Her muscles tightened around her fingers, which were soaked and buried deep inside her.

Still she doubted this was how Marc would make her come. She pictured him as a man, his blue eyes tinted with hints of silver. Just imagining him set her soul on fire. So wild, a cop with a raw edge to him, and definitely more man than she'd ever known before.

Already he'd pushed her boundaries, seen straight through her when she'd been at his house. Within minutes, he'd made demands of her, insisting on complete honesty. And she hadn't even realized until he kicked her out that she was lying to him.

What would he do to her if he fucked her?

Her fingers weren't enough. Glancing around her room, her mind fogged with lust and images of Marc torturing her, she noticed her hairbrush on her desk and reached for it. Using the handle, she pressed it against her soaked pussy, feeling its hardness slowly move inside her.

"Oh, hell yes." She bit her lip, sliding down in the chair so that she could move the brush handle in and out of her cunt.

The bristles of the brush pushed against her palm but she didn't care. And the handle wasn't long enough. It didn't reach that spot inside her that ached for relief. Imagining Marc naked, remembering how he had looked when he transformed at the edge of the woods the other night, sent her over the edge.

His cock hadn't been hard, but she pretended she held it in her hand. She would make it as hard as the brush handle, and ease it inside her. He would be able to fuck her until she screamed.

And he'd push her, make demands of her that she wouldn't think to do on her own. Just the thought of what he might make her do made her hot. Everything about Marc terrified her, and sent a thrill of excitement rushing through her.

She began pounding the handle in and out of her, moving as fast as she could while her orgasm seeped through her. It wasn't the climax she needed, but a small amount of relief crept through her.

"Damn it," she sighed, pulling her hairbrush out of her and staring at the cream-covered handle. "What are you going to do with yourself?"

Her legs were wobbly when she stood, her mind still tormented with images of Marc. The way he'd looked when he'd opened his door earlier, not wearing a shirt, and with that chest hair that was just begging her to run her fingers through it—damn.

She would be head over heels in trouble with Marc McAllister in her life.

Chapter Six

❦

Marc stared at his coffee table where the manila file still rested from the night before. It had been a long day at work, and even after showering, he still felt an air of gloom around him.

Stone, his youngest brother, had called him earlier inviting him over to enjoy their kill. "All the rowdies will be here so leave your cop hat at home," he'd said jokingly on the phone.

Neither of his brothers had any sense of responsibility in their lives and they both seemed happy as could be. They were decent and hard-working, but nonetheless still pups. As much as he'd prefer to spend the evening alone, he'd agreed to come over. Maybe some downtime would help clear his head. And as much as they referred to themselves as rowdy, Marc knew they weren't law breakers.

It's going to take a lot more than downtime to get Heather Graham out of your head.

And there was her article, taunting him silently as it rested on his coffee table. He walked over and picked it up, immediately detecting her scent on it.

Those deep green eyes of hers appeared in his thoughts, so guarded, yet so full of emotion and curiosity. She ached to know him, and she wanted him. The desire surrounding her couldn't be missed. It was a wonderful scent on her, such a rich, sweet smell. His insides hardened thinking about her.

Damn, he wanted to see her again.

Opening the file, he stared down at the neatly typed pages. FIRST DRAFT was centered at the top of the page. He glanced down, reading the first paragraph, and then skimming down the page.

Humans that can change into monsters live among us. Werewolves have walked among us for centuries. All of the myths are true. They terrify us yet they beg us not to be scared. This reporter decided to mix among these werewolves, discover the truth of how dangerous these mutated creatures could be.

Marc gripped the file so hard that several of the pages slipped free, and floated to the floor around them.

"Mutated creatures, my ass!" He couldn't believe that was what she really thought.

The manila file began crumpling, the thick paper crunching against his grip. The little bitch needed quite an education.

"She wants to mix among werewolves, does she?" he said through gritted teeth.

He hurled the file across the room then stormed out of his house. It was a Friday night, but the thought that she might have plans didn't cross his mind until he pulled up in front of her apartment complex and didn't see her car. Nonetheless, he stormed up to the door he'd seen her enter the night before and knocked none too quietly.

His temper didn't subside any when no one answered. Well, he would find Miss Heather Graham. And just to seal the deal, he put in a quick call to his brothers, informing them he would be bringing a date.

Now, to track down the adorable little bitch, and tracking people was something he did very well.

After a quick drive through town, scanning the parking lots of the restaurants on the main strip, he didn't spot her car. Images of what he might do if he found her out on a date popped into his head.

She would be with him tonight. He'd set his mind to it. Heather needed an education. He would be damned to hell if that article he'd just scanned ever saw the light of day. And in her own words she wanted to know about werewolves. Well she was damn sure going to learn about them, and she was going to learn the truth.

He'd almost given thought to calling out the pack, putting out a search for her, when he drove by a small coffee shop and spotted her car parked on the street.

Gotcha!

Parking across the street, he took long, anxious paces, not slowing when he entered the shop. Ignoring the young woman who greeted him at the counter, he scanned the dimly lit shop filled with humans, until he spotted a group in a booth along the wall.

Heather's scent stood out easily among the rest. He moved with the silence of the predator, until he was at the edge of the table. Several women about Heather's age looked up, their gazes strolling over him with mild curiosity.

"Hi there," one of them said with a flirty smile.

He ignored her too.

Heather sat at the outside of the booth, which was a damned good thing. He'd hate to have to drag her over the table. Taking her arm, he lifted her out of her seat.

One surprised Heather Graham looked up at him wide-eyed. "What the hell?" she asked.

He pulled a ten out of his pocket and dropped it on the table. "I hope this covers your part of the tab. You're coming with me."

"Heather? Who is this?" Another woman began to stand.

Marc didn't offer any of them any explanation.

"It's okay. I'll call you later." Heather did her best to turn and wave to her friends, but he didn't slow his pace in leading her out the door.

Heather didn't protest as he guided the way out of the coffee shop, noting little alarm in the emotions of the humans sitting at the different tables. These people didn't care about each other, had no compassion for anyone other than themselves. And she referred to his kind as the monsters.

The cold night air did little to calm the fire burning inside him. He didn't let go of Heather's arm until they'd reached her car.

"You can drive your car back to your apartment, or leave it here. But either way, you're with me tonight."

Heather blinked, looking up at him while she seemed to take time to digest his words. "Is this the way a werewolf asks a lady out on a date?"

If that was amusement in her gaze, it faded quickly the longer she looked at him. His own rage filled the air, smelling like rotten fruit, and it made it difficult to sniff out her emotions.

"When I ask you out on date, you'll know it." He managed to curb his anger, forcing his insides to relax. Hairs prickled on the back of his neck, his carnal nature aching to come forth. Letting out a slow breath, he continued, "That article you wrote is trash. Not a word of it will appear before the public. If you indeed want to learn about werewolves, your education starts now."

Heather's tongue darted over her lips. She looked up at him, her green eyes alight with fire. Just gazing at her calmed him down. He wasn't sure he liked the power she was gaining on him. And he would be damned if he let her know that she'd gotten under his skin.

Arousal mixed with defiance peppered the air with a rich scent that drowned out the small amount of perfume she wore. He noticed too that tonight she sported sleek leggings and a short sweater, showing off her narrow waistline and slim hips.

Reminding himself that she was human, her petite frame proof of how fragile she was, he fought his emotions even further.

Heather glanced at her car, and then down the street past him. "What did you have in mind?"

"We're going to a small party, a werewolf gathering."

The excitement that lit her face was all the proof he needed to see that she was up for the adventure. His emotions calmed even further when he saw how spending the evening with him pleased her.

"I accept your invitation." She turned toward her car, and with her back to him added, "But I'm not the only one who needs an education."

He stayed on her ass while she drove through town and back to her apartment. He was glad to see she was willing to drive with him, that she trusted him enough to allow him to escort her. He'd told her the other night that he would never hurt her, and he'd meant it.

Heather parked her car and got out, crossing her arms over her chest. "Am I dressed okay for this party of yours?"

He let his gaze drop down her. "You look damn good to me."

A small smile crossed her face, the fresh scent of happiness filling the air around her. She didn't move when he got out of the car. He slipped his arm around her, letting his fingers stray down her back, and then cupped her soft ass when he guided her around to the passenger door.

She turned before he could open the door for her. "Don't get any ideas, Marc McAllister. I'm going with you for the education, remember that."

He gripped her ass, pulling her to him, and then nibbled on her lower lip before she could stop him. "And an education is what you're going to get," he told her, and then pulled her in closer, needing to taste more of her.

When she relaxed into him, her body curving along his as she arched her back, giving what he demanded, his entire body turned rock-hard. More than anything he could devour her right here and now. Nothing had ever tasted so sweet. No woman had ever curved into him so perfectly.

A growl escaped him, his heart pumping furiously, blood rushing through him while his cock turned to stone.

"Marc," she cried out, breaking off the kiss when she turned her head and gasped for air.

He could feast on her all night. And he just might do that.

Letting her go, he turned her around and opened the car door, giving her adorable ass a slight swat. "Get in," he said, enjoying her disgruntled expression.

It didn't take too long to drive out of town. He took his time driving along Hart Highway, enjoying the wonderful night sky that spread out before him. A run would be perfect later that evening. He needed to be out under this sky, feeling the crisp night air around him.

Once they reached Wright Creek Road he sensed Heather getting nervous. This would be good for her, and he knew she would be safe among his den and their friends. Pulling into the long drive that led back to the small cabin he'd lived in with his brothers up until recently, he parked among several other familiar cars.

"This is where my den lives," he told her, enjoying how her eyes brightened in the dark with a mixture of curiosity and a bit of fear.

She got out on her own, and stood at the front of the car for a moment without following him toward the house. He turned, reaching for her when she hesitated.

"Remember what I told you," he whispered, brushing his mouth over the warmth of her forehead, inhaling the perfumed scent of her shampoo. "I will never allow you to be hurt. Do you believe me?"

"Yes," she nodded, looking up at him. "I believe you."

Nonetheless, her nervousness increased when he opened the front door and led her in to his brother's den, a mixture of rock music and the smell of beer greeting them.

Heather's knees wobbled underneath her when she followed Marc into the small cabin. She was greeted by laughter coming from another room, and the enticing smell of barbeque.

The way Marc had yanked her away from her friends still had her rattled. Men just didn't act like that, and that fact that he did, that he'd practically dragged her out of the café like a caveman would his woman, was beyond unbelievable. Men simply didn't act like that. With all of her research on werewolves, she knew they were more aggressive than humans, but dragging her out?

He'd thrown her so off-guard, she hadn't been able to think straight. But then he'd told her she was with him tonight, that they were going to a werewolf party, and all because he wanted to show her how werewolves really were.

Damn. If only he'd realized she'd gotten one hell of an education right there in the coffee shop. Werewolves were definitely more primitive than humans.

And she should be pissed at him for his actions. And she would be. As soon as she got over being pissed at herself for being so damned turned on by how he treated her.

She took a look around the small home that looked the way she'd picture any home would look with two young men living in it. The furniture was secondhand. There were little to no wall hangings. And a couple of open bottles of beer sat on the box crate that posed as a coffee table in front of the couch.

There was nothing to be nervous about, she told herself. Nonetheless, her heart pounded in her chest. This was a home full of werewolves, and they had all their friends over. They would know she was human.

Her heart skipped a beat.

She couldn't have asked for a better occasion to be taken to. The fact that Marc had offered, wanted her to see how they lived, was almost too good to be true. It hurt that he called her article trash, but she should have expected that. She was writing about his people from a human perspective. Of course there were areas she needed to tighten up, but she hoped tonight would give her that extra punch she felt her article needed.

"Marc. There you are." A young man entered from another room, a smaller version of Marc, and she guessed, one of his brothers. "And this must be the date you mentioned."

Then the man paused, looking at her, his smile fading. He glanced from her, to Marc, and wrinkled his brow. Heather licked her lips, something akin to panic rushing through her.

Marc took her hand, and the man lowered his gaze, watching the act.

"Stone, this is Heather Graham. Be nice and say hi." There was a warning in his tone she didn't miss.

"You could have told us you were bringing a human." Stone gave her the once-over, his brow wrinkling under blond bangs that fell almost to his eyes. "Come on in though. Hope you like your meat rare."

Stone turned without another word, his muscular stance probably quite a turn-on with women his age. He wore a white muscle T-shirt that tucked into faded blue jeans. Worn cowboy boots finished the ensemble. It was obvious he and Marc were brothers, the family resemblance very noticeable. She felt like a midget next to these blond giants.

Marc let go of her hand, placing his hand on her lower back, and gave her a gentle push. His touch was protective though, and she found herself not wanting him to take his hand off of her when they followed the young man, Stone — what kind of name was that? — into the kitchen.

A handful of people, in the middle of laughing, all paused and gave her their full attention when she and Marc joined them.

"Everyone, this is Heather. Play nice, or else."

Damn it. He had to warn them to be nice to her?

Heather stared around at the cluttered kitchen, full with a handful of people who all stopped what they were doing to give her their undivided attention. Never had she felt more exposed in all of her life.

They all looked like normal people. And if Marc hadn't told her beforehand, she wouldn't have known any of them were werewolves.

Four men and three women, ranging in age from college to a bit older than she, all gave her a curious once-over. The oldest-looking woman, a lady about her age who was damned good-looking, was the first to move. Stepping forward, she stuck out her hand.

"Well, any friend of Marc's is a friend of ours." The woman's smile seemed friendly enough. She wore a fair amount of makeup and sported a blue denim miniskirt, loose-fitting blouse, and black hose with flat boots. "I'm Simone. Welcome to the McAllister den."

With that, the woman nudged the younger man next to her, who jumped, as if he'd just remembered it was his turn to speak.

"Yeah, welcome." He took his turn shaking her hand. His grip was firm, but his hand a lot cooler than the woman's. "I'm Gabe, Marc's brother. Sorry we're a bit stunned. We don't get many humans out this way."

Again Marc pulled her to him, making a silent statement that they were definitely a date that night. Heather didn't miss the curiosity that swarmed on all of their faces. It wasn't too surprising. If she'd taken him out with her, and introduced him as a werewolf, it would stupefy her friends.

She straightened, hoping they would see she could carry her own weight. "And it's not every day I enter a house full of werewolves," she said, grinning at Gabe.

Gabe gave her a sincere smile in return. She guessed he was probably in his mid-twenties, a little bit more of a redhead than his brothers, although streaks of blond were visible. His hair was longer, falling past the collar of his plaid shirt, which was unbuttoned halfway down a massive chest that was thick with hair. The shirt was untucked, hanging over worn jeans that showed off long, muscular legs. He too wore worn cowboy boots.

Dear Lord. The McAllister men were sexy as hell. She imagined Marc's younger brothers were probably at least as unruly as he was. Their mother must have been a saint to deal with these three.

"Heather, this is Rock, Simone's mate," Marc said, pointing out a man who stood as tall as Marc, and didn't smile or offer his hand, but simply nodded at her.

She didn't catch the names of the younger women, who giggled through their introductions, and were obviously more interested in Marc's brothers than they were her. When Gabe, who was obviously the one with manners in the room, introduced the older guy who leaned against the counter, he was introduced to Marc as well as her.

"Bastien Rousseau just came back from overseas," Gabe explained, his attention on Marc. "Rock here was telling him that he might have work for him out on his ranch."

The conversation picked back up with talk about work, and Heather slowly relaxed, although found herself hovering close to Marc. Between Marc and his brothers, as well as the quiet werewolf, Rock, she felt like she was in a room of giants. Bastien was a lot smaller than the other men, slim-built, but uninhibited by his size.

Once again the kitchen filled with lots of laughter and conversation, and she felt like she'd been forgotten.

Stone said something about checking on the meat out back, and Marc turned to her, giving her a wink, and then left her standing in the kitchen with the other women when he left through sliding glass doors into the darkness of the night outside.

The college girls whispered and giggled amongst themselves, and then left in a huddle to follow the men, leaving her alone with the way too pretty Simone who crossed her arms and focused a serious gaze on her.

Heather straightened, feeling she was getting ready for a showdown.

"I'm not sure what you think you're doing getting involved with a *Cariboo*. But most *lunewulf* can't handle them. I know a human can't." Simone spoke so casually her words almost didn't sound insulting.

Heather decided the best approach here would be honesty.

She straightened. "I'm a reporter, working on an article about werewolves. Marc offered to bring me out here to learn more about you."

Simone raised an eyebrow, her thoughts on the matter not clear by her expression. "Beer?" she asked.

"That would be nice."

Simone pulled a bottle from the refrigerator, and then brought the cap to her mouth. Heather watched in awe as Simone's front teeth grew longer, and she pulled the cap free from the bottle, then spat it into the trash can. She handed the bottle to Heather.

No way in hell would this woman intimidate her.

Heather took the bottle, nodding her thanks, and took a long gulp.

"Neat trick," she said, unable to keep herself from glancing outside where the men were.

Simone crossed her arms over her chest, her look intent as if she was about to do the interviewing. "So your interests in Marc are purely professional."

"I'm a reporter. My entire life is purely professional." Commenting that she was more than aware that Marc was sexy as hell seemed pointless.

Simone shook her head. "You're in over your head, darlin'," she said, sounding apologetic. "Do you even know the difference between *Cariboo* and *lunewulf*?"

Heather chewed her lip. She'd heard there were different breeds of werewolves, but decided picking this woman's brain wouldn't hurt.

"Why don't you enlighten me?"

"Those men out there are *Cariboo*. All except Bastien. They are wild, untameable, and very, very aggressive." She let her gaze run down Heather. "You wouldn't last one night with him."

Heather took another drink of her beer, suddenly very thirsty. Thoughts of how he'd pulled her away from her friends earlier came to mind. Marc took what he wanted, that much was clear. She had a feeling she would find out soon enough what a night with him would be like. The thought made the room way too warm.

"You might be right."

"I know I am."

"Well then, maybe I should just go an hour with him at first."

Simone simply stared at her for a minute, and then broke out laughing, a deep, almost husky sound. "You're okay, girl," she said, giving Heather a slap on the back. "But I doubt he'd let you go after just an hour."

"Damn." Heather looked toward the sliding glass door again, the men's voices loud and boisterous outside.

Without warning, the glass door slid open quickly, the rich smell of barbeque filling the room as the men paraded in.

"Care to share in our kill?" Stone asked her, his teeth longer than they should be as he ripped part of a steak off in his mouth and chewed greedily while grinning at her.

They ended up outside, eating steak which most of them simply held in their hands, chewing at greedily. She was grateful when Marc found a plate and fork and steak knife for her, and gave her a not quite so rare piece.

Hardly any meat was left by the time they'd finished — an entire deer had been successfully eaten. And Heather had to admit, the steaks and beer hit the spot. She watched with a bit of caution when Gabe and Stone went at it in the backyard, or rather untamed land outside the cabin. The surroundings fit the McAllister men perfectly.

She jumped when Rock leapt at the two men, and threw Stone halfway across the open area, before thick trees started.

"Don't let him bully you, Stone," Simone cheered them on.

Stone came back at them, his clothes ripping when his body began changing. Heather realized she'd taken a step backwards and into Marc's arms when the men changed, and suddenly three very large and dangerous werewolves growled at each other in the night.

"They're just having a bit of fun," Marc whispered, his hands snaking around her waist while he nipped at her neck.

The smell of beer on his breath and the way his hands came dangerously close to her breasts, reminded her of the words Simone said earlier. The night air no longer seemed as chilly.

Her mouth went dry though when Simone ripped off her shirt, displaying two very large and perfectly shaped breasts. She turned and grinned a toothy grin at them.

"You going to run with us, Marc? Or stay here and fuck her?" Her voice garbled as she spoke, her body slowly changing as she stripped off her skirt and stockings.

Heather realized at that moment that this was the life of a werewolf. At night they ran under the stars, enjoying the freedom of freeing the beast within them. She could only imagine if she encouraged Marc to stay with her, all that pent-up energy might be used on her. Thoughts of how rough he might be fucking her made her body boil with need. But she wouldn't deprive him of being who he was.

"Go run with them," she whispered, turning her head so she could look up at him. "I'll wait for you here."

His blue eyes glowed with silver. Marc was so huge, so muscular and hard. His cock sprang to life while he looked down at her. It pressed against her backside, a promise of what she could have later. He slipped his hand inside the back of her leggings, his skin rough and hot as he cupped her bare ass.

"Yes. You will wait for me. Your education has barely started." He turned her around, his hand sliding from her ass to her front and he cupped her shaved pussy. "Fucking shit, woman," he growled, and then nipped at her lip when he pulled her to him.

His cock was rock-hard, eager and determined and she about came on his hand when he thrust a finger deep inside her.

As quickly as he'd grabbed her, he pushed her to arm's length and let go of her. His expression bordered on dangerous while he stared at her, never looking away while he removed his clothes.

Heather couldn't speak, couldn't breathe. Seeing him naked again, when he'd just had his finger deep in her cunt, made her world spin around her. When he stripped out of his jeans, his cock appeared twice the size it had been the last time she'd seen him naked. Hard and swollen, it jutted out toward her, looking as demanding and determined as the rest of him.

Suddenly her mouth was too wet, thoughts of what he could do to her with that making her weak in the knees. Her blood pulsed so hard through her that her ears rang, and she wished for somewhere to sit, something to hold onto. Anything to stabilize herself while she gawked at the incredibly sexy man who stood before her.

And then slowly, never taking his gaze from her, he began to change. His body transformed, shoulders altering, fur appearing over his skin, his body contorting. She saw his facial muscles harden and wondered if the change hurt him.

In the next instant he fell to all fours, making her jump when he let out a powerful howl.

"Holy shit!" she screamed when he leapt over her.

Her heart about exploded in her chest and she turned in time to see him leap after the others, and disappear into the trees beyond the yard.

Heather was left alone, stranded at a small cabin outside of town.

Chapter Seven

🕭

Marc tore at the earth, his powerful claws ripping the ground without mercy as he raced across the open field with the others. Letting go, pushing himself as hard as he could, feeling his muscles strain at the pace they kept, felt damned good.

It had taken too much restraint on his part not to fuck Heather right there behind his brother's house. No one would have stopped him, especially Heather. The sweet smell of desire on her still fogged his senses. He loved when a bitch kept her pussy clean and shaven. And Heather's cunt had been so smooth, so wet.

His dick hardened, making it harder to keep up with the others. But he couldn't keep his mind off of Heather. Knowing she would be there when he returned made his blood boil. Forcing himself to pay attention, desperately needing to burn off some energy so he wouldn't hurt Heather when he returned, he pushed ahead.

He'd promised her that he would never hurt her, and he'd meant it. But thoughts of tearing her clothes off of her with his teeth, plunging deep into that hot, wet cunt of hers, had the blood boiling through his veins.

The cold air slapped at his face. Moisture clung to his coat, feeding him, making him feel more alive as he raced with the others. No matter how chilly the night was, he still burned with need. He leapt forward, aching to rid some of the raw energy that pulsed inside him.

The *lunewulf* were much smaller, but Simone and Bastien had no problem keeping up with the others. Speed was their asset, and Simone was the first to leap over a rambling creek when they came up on it. The others followed suit.

Marc leapt into the air, his muscles rippling under his dew-moistened coat. He hit the ground hard, tearing at the earth with his claws, laughing and howling with the others.

The air around them was thick with the smell of moist grass, rich soil, and cold water. If he weren't stuffed from the meat he would enjoy catching a few fish. The deeper ponds around them were full of them. He could hear them splashing through the water, hurrying to get away from the deadly predators that tore through the night.

Rock was the first to slow, his alert expression and deep bark alerting the others.

We're not alone.

Marc turned, surprised to see the single headlight bouncing over the terrain behind them. The dirt bike slowed, its rider hesitating. Growls came from his den mates and friends, as they all stopped, turning to face the rider who dared to interrupt their run.

The rider came to a stop, the dirt bike's engine sputtering, disturbing the peace of the night.

"Marc?" a nervous Heather called out.

He couldn't fucking believe his ears. Prancing forward until he could see Heather sitting on the bike, pride soared through him like he'd never experienced before. She'd come after him.

The others moved in on her, slowly circling her while she stared at all of them nervously. Marc strutted up to his brother's dirt bike, amused to see her wearing Stone's leather jacket. She about drowned in it. But damn, who would have thought his little reporter bitch could ride a dirt bike?

"I'm not stealing anything," she said, glancing around at the werewolves who had circled her, watching her with amusement. "I...I just didn't want to be left out."

Marc pressed his nose into her, burrowing inside his brother's leather coat so that he could inhale her scent.

"Can I ride alongside you while you run?" she asked quietly, so only he could hear over the rumble of the engine.

He ran his tongue over her knuckles, her hands wrapped around the throttle. Her flesh was cold and the thought that he would make her body gleam with sweat later sent a furious fever burning through him.

He threw his head back, unable to contain himself, and let out a howl that tore free of his body, sending all small creatures within hearing distance running for cover.

The night was his. Never had he felt more power, more absolute freedom than he did at that moment. Tearing off to lead his pack of friends, he felt more alive than he had in ages.

The others followed suit, the run once again picking up pace. This time however, Heather matched them on the old dirt bike, impressing the hell out of him with her expertise. She splashed through the small creeks, not deterred by the rocky ground, as she kept pace and tore over the ground alongside him.

After an hour or so, he veered off, needing to be alone with her. Heather had impressed him more than he thought possible.

The others didn't question him when he broke away, leaping the other direction when they'd reached the northern end of Rock's land. Heather followed him, not hesitating but rumbling after him on the small bike. He slowed when he knew they were alone.

Heather brought the bike to a stop, and actually laughed when she climbed off of it. "I haven't ridden a bike in years," she said, her face glowing with a happiness he had yet to see on her. "I brought your clothes," she added, more quietly, her hesitation returning.

Marc let the change ripple through him, the darkness around him becoming blacker as he took his human form.

Suddenly it was colder, his surroundings less clear, as his human senses disabled him from enjoying the wondrous smells of the night.

"How thoughtful of you," he said, pulling her to him and stripping his brother's heavy jacket from her.

There was no way he could contain himself. More than he needed to breathe, he needed to be buried deep inside her.

"Marc," she cried out, although not fighting him when he reached for her sweater, quickly pulling it over her head.

Laying it over the seat of the bike—his thoughts clear enough at least to know if he'd thrown her clothes on the ground they would be damp within minutes from the dew on the ground—he reached for her leggings next.

"There's nothing to lay down on," she whispered, her voice suddenly husky as she filled the air around them with her wonderfully sweet smell of desire and need. "And...and it's cold."

"I'll keep you warm."

He wasn't sure how he managed to get her boots off of her, but he needed her naked, needed to feel her against him. Damn it. He needed to be inside her, deep inside her—now.

The moon and stars offered enough light to make her flesh glow. Emerald eyes looked up at him with wonder, her breasts rising and falling as she took in deep breaths. Her tummy was flat, her waist so damned slender. And he could smell her lust when he gazed on her shaven mound, so beautiful.

She nervously ran her small fingers through her hair, pushing it away from her face, while her tongue brushed over her lips.

Marc couldn't wait another minute.

He reached for her, pulling her into his arms, feeling her breasts press against him. Burying his face in her strawberry-blonde hair, he inhaled her scent, letting it fill him, everything about him becoming Heather Graham.

Even her human scent appealed to him. He wondered at that, knowing he never would have believed it if someone were to tell him he would fall for a human. And he realized that was what he was doing. It was more than trying to ensure that she didn't slander his kind in the newspaper. No longer did it seem important that he show this saucy little bitch what it was like to be a werewolf. He needed to show her what it was like to know him.

She was impressive, showing she could live on the wild side, take on life and embrace it. Heather was up for an adventure, exploring the new and unknown and embracing it. Her excitement toward life and what it had to offer showed in the way she'd sought him out while on his run.

Marc reached under her arms, lifting her, pulling her up his body until her face was level to his.

"Wrap your arms around me, little bitch," he muttered, his body hardening painfully when her nipples scraped over his flesh.

Heather bit her lower lip, staring at him, while she carefully wrapped her arms around his neck. Without instruction, her legs went around his waist, her moist cunt sliding down against his swollen cock.

He cupped her ass, holding her, guiding her while he slowly penetrated into her heat.

Marc was sure his entire world would explode right before his eyes. He'd never imagined her to be so fucking tight.

"Please tell me you aren't a virgin," he groaned, the thought suddenly crossing his mind.

Heather's expression turned pouty and the change in her scent told him he'd offended her.

"I'm not a virgin." Her voice was strained.

He filled her, stretching her muscles, feeling her heat rush through him making his world spin out of control around him.

Holding her, pinning her to him, he glided deeper.

Heather cried out, her head falling back as she bucked against him. There was no way Marc would let go of her. Lifting her slightly so that her soaked muscles shifted over his shaft, he allowed her the slightest respite before burying himself deep inside of her again.

Heather's nails dug deep into his shoulders. The sweet pain egged him on, and he held on tightly to her soft ass while he lifted and slammed her down on his cock.

She barely weighed anything and was so easy to push into. After a few minutes, her body adjusted to him, her heat soaring through him while he moved her body, and she held on to him for dear life.

With her arms and legs wrapped around him, he stood in the meadow, raising her off of his cock and then allowing her to slide down his shaft again. She arched into him, holding on with stretched arms while her head fell back.

Her body tightened when he'd get about three quarters of his cock inside her. Maybe she wasn't a virgin, but she hadn't fucked often, and it had been a while since she'd been with a man. That knowledge appealed to him. Heather would be his, and every time he plummeted deep into her tight heat, he was claiming a bit more of her.

His cock grew, her heat forcing the blood to pump through him at a dangerous rate. He fought not to change, to remain completely human for her, even though the creature inside him screamed for release.

His muscles ached to grow, while his cock swelled, thickening as he buried himself in her.

"Holy shit!" She twisted in his arms when he went exceptionally deep, finally filling her completely with all he had to offer.

She shook her head from side to side, while her breasts bounced to the point of distraction when he moved her over him faster.

"This is…too…much…" Her breath came in pants, and he was sure he'd have scratch marks on his shoulders when they were done.

Not that he cared a bit.

But he did know her body was fragile, and he had no desire to hurt her. Slowing the momentum, he buried himself one last time, enjoying how her body convulsed when she came. Her head came forward, her eyes a beautiful shade of emerald, her cheeks flushed a deep red, and her mouth forming an adorable circle.

She exploded over his cock, her muscles convulsing around him, milking him. He released deep inside her, holding her ass firmly in place while a growl that turned into a howl escaped him.

Heather fell forward, collapsing in his arms, and he moved to cradle her there, enjoying the moment while his cock remained firmly locked inside her.

"I think you just killed me," she whispered, and then attempted a laugh.

"I think you're more alive now than maybe you ever have been," he whispered back, content to hold her there for as long as possible.

Chapter Eight

ഔ

Heather had never been more miserable at work. It had been dawn when Marc finally dropped her off at her apartment.

"I'll call you later today," he'd told her, and then had pulled her to him for a deep, intoxicating kiss.

And that had been the last she'd seen him. The rest of the weekend, try as she would to work on her article, Marc distracted her thoughts. He consumed her dreams too. Monday morning showed up way too quickly.

She was jittery from all the coffee she'd downed just trying to make it to lunch. And now with storms pending, it looked like she was being sent out on assignment. At least she wouldn't be stuck at her desk trying to stay awake throughout the day.

"I thought you might be interested in this one," Stephen Boswell told her, stepping into the coffee room where Heather stood eagerly waiting for a fresh pot to percolate.

His brown suit hung on him crookedly. Stephen had never been one to focus on his own appearance. He was a damn good editor though. "Some of the werewolves are meeting down at City Hall. Something about petitioning for their own school. I guess they think they're too good for us, huh?"

Heather glanced at the fax he held out to her. Just the mention of werewolves sent her insides into lustful turmoil. No matter that she was tired as hell, more sore than she'd ever been in her life, not to mention grumpy from no sleep—the mention of anything having remotely to do with Marc had her insides throbbing.

Dear Lord. She must be a glutton for punishment wanting more of that wild man again so soon.

"I'll head down there." Maybe information on werewolves that had nothing to do with Marc might help with her article. She needed to keep her thoughts unbiased. "Thanks."

She turned and walked out of the room, forgetting about her coffee. Already she wondered if she might see Marc down at the courthouse. After all, something like this might require the law to step in.

"Hey." Stephen tapped her arm with his stubby fingers. "You look like shit."

"Thanks." She waved over her shoulder, not wanting to discuss her dark circles under her eyes. At least he couldn't see the sore muscles that ached throughout her body. "Rough weekend."

She still couldn't believe she'd had the nerve to pull that old dirt bike out from the side of the cabin Friday night. It had been years, since she was a teenager, since she'd ridden. Her ass and inner thighs had been tingling for hours after getting off of that thing.

Heather had given up all of her tomboy antics when she'd headed off to college. If she wanted to make it as a big-shot reporter, no one could know about her small-town life, or her humble upbringing. She'd left all that behind for the city lights and the glamour, and look where it had her at the moment, too damned tired to even laugh about it.

Things were even more out of hand when Heather and her photographer, Joey, arrived at City Hall. Large drops of rain splattered on Heather's silk blouse, which had been the first thing she'd grabbed when stumbling through her morning routine so she'd make it to work on time. She hurried through the crowd, following Joey inside.

"Give me a second to get rolling." Joey had worked with her for over a year now, and had a gift for catching some award-winning photographs.

The two of them made a damn good team usually. They'd been assigned to work together right after he'd been hired on by the paper. At the time, she'd been insulted, being given some young pup fresh out of college as her photographer. But since she was one of the few reporters who actually had her own photographer, she didn't bitch. Heather blinked hard, her eyes burning with fatigue as she looked down at the notes she'd quickly scribbled to bring her up to date with what was going on.

"Where's your cheat book on werewolves?" Joey asked, his camera strapped around his neck. Already he was taking off his lens cap.

Tall and skinny, with long, straight brown hair that he always kept in a ponytail, Joey gave her his "let's go get them" smile. He had way too much energy today.

And she was all thumbs. A major story was breaking here. Damn. Damn. Damn.

"It's in my bag." She almost dropped her shoulder bag that she hauled everywhere when working. Finding her black, three-ring binder, she quickly flipped through the pages. "Okay. Here is their pack leader. See him anywhere around?"

With a quick glance at the picture of Johann Rousseau, Joey scanned the crowd.

"There he is," he said, and then almost dragged her through the large foyer where everyone talking was echoing loudly all around them.

She fumbled for her handheld recorder when she spotted a man matching the picture. "Johann Rousseau, one question, please?" she asked, holding the recorder in front of him.

"I don't have any comments at this time."

"How can humans help your werewolves get their own school?"

Joey almost dropped his camera when he looked at her like she was nuts. Johann stopped, giving her a careful once-over. Aware that he could smell out her emotions, she took a slow, deep breath, and hoped she managed a pleasant smile. She'd just gained the pack leader's undivided attention.

"Have we met before?" he asked, looking distracted.

"Heather Graham with the *Prince George Tribune*. I'd appreciate any comments you might have time to offer."

A man next to Johann whispered something in his ear, and Heather stood with bated breath, praying Marc's name wasn't being mentioned. But no one could confirm what had happened the night before.

"I've seen no indication that humans want to help us in this matter, Miss Graham." Johann was a good-looking man, with an easygoing manner. He smiled pleasantly when Joey snapped his picture.

Dressed casually in a button-down shirt and black jeans, she would never have guessed him a werewolf. He certainly wasn't as big as Marc. But then she doubted any man or werewolf could come close to being as big as Marc.

"There isn't funding for another school, and you know it," someone yelled from off to the side.

"But their kids are destroying our school. They are animals and shouldn't be allowed in our town."

Heather scanned the crowd growing around her, while Joey let his camera angle toward whoever had just spoken. His flash went off repeatedly.

"The werewolves are taking over our town," someone else yelled.

"Why don't you want your werewolves in our schools?" One of her main competitors stuck his handheld tape recorder in Johann's face.

Johann glared at the man. His tone remained calm though. "We aren't asking for city funding, just the right to purchase land to build our own school."

"Give them the land and get them away from us," someone chanted.

"Can you tell us how cubs are different from human children?" Heather asked.

"You're sounding like you're sympathetic to their cause," Joey hissed in her ear.

"We don't want them in our schools anyway," someone else yelled.

"They shouldn't even be in City Hall," someone else yelled.

There was some shoving behind her, and Heather fought to maintain her footing when she about fell into the pack leader.

Joey was snapping his camera furiously, but someone fell into him. Heather hit the stone wall hard, the pain riveting through her shoulder, and dropped her microphone.

"This is ridiculous," she heard Johann say.

She grabbed his arm. "Grant me an interview," she said, and then he was pulled away from her by several men surrounding him.

"Do you deny the fact that fighting among the children has increased eighty percent since your werewolves have started going to our schools?" she heard someone ask.

Remembering how Marc's younger brothers had scrapped in their backyard the night before, she didn't doubt it. Rubbing her shoulder and willing the pain away, she tried to get her bearings in the ever-growing crowd that was obviously turning mean.

A quick glance at the growing crowd inside City Hall, and she noticed several police officers ordering people to calm down. Immediately she tried to find Marc, but Joey was grabbing her arm.

"Come on, their leader is headed this way." He grabbed her arm and dragged her through the foyer full of people.

They were just behind Johann when he disappeared into one of the meeting rooms and the doors were closed behind him.

"If they get the city to give them money to build their school, we'll tie it up in court for years," a man bellowed loudly behind her.

Heather turned as another person spoke.

"I don't see why you want their kind with our children anyway. They could change and attack our kids." The woman who spoke sounded close to tears.

"As long as they don't get a nicer school than ours," someone else yelled.

"Next thing you know they'll be running for office."

Heather stuck her microphone in the face of one of the men who had been with Johann before he entered the room. "Do you see any of your pack running for city positions?" she asked.

"I think it would help in getting us fairly represented," he answered.

"After all, there are as many of us as there are of you," another werewolf spoke up. "In fact, we were here first."

"Like hell you were," someone shouted.

Heather wasn't sure who threw the first punch. She didn't have time to react when suddenly she found herself in the middle of a brawl. Falling to the ground, doing her best to protect her recorder and microphone, she scrambled out of the way.

Large hands grabbed her, and before she could react, she was being dragged backwards, quickly.

She was outside the building before she had a chance to regain her footing. Marc almost leapt down the front stairs of City Hall with her in his arms.

"Your day is done. Go home. Now." He looked fierce, every muscle in his body taut, as if he would pounce without a moment's notice.

Wearing his cop uniform, it looked like his body might explode out of his clothing at any minute. His expression was hard, his lips pursed while deep blue eyes devoured her. She sucked in her breath, unable to pull her gaze from him.

Heather straightened her shirt, half-checking that she wasn't injured and to make sure she still had her tape recorder and all of her other stuff. Going home sounded damn good to her. But she needed to be here. There was a breaking story going on inside that building. Not only would it help her with her article, but she could make the front page if she could tap this story.

At the moment, protesting to Marc didn't appear to be in her best interest.

Joey came hurrying down the stairs of the building, looking worried and anxious.

"Thanks, officer," he said to Marc, barely acknowledging him as he reached for Heather. "I think if we head around the back side of the building, we can catch the werewolves there. I bet they leave that way."

"Heather." Marc's growl wasn't ignored by either one of them.

Joey looked at him, puzzled. Heather cleared her throat, her heart suddenly pounding too hard in her chest.

"I still have some work to do here." No man, or werewolf, was going to bully her.

"I just told you to go home." Marc didn't look away from her, narrowing her world down to just the two of them.

The rain started falling harder, and she knew her silk blouse clung to her. She hadn't even thought to grab an umbrella, and she had a feeling her lace bra was easily seen through the material of her shirt.

"What did she do wrong, officer?" Joey asked, stuffing his camera under his shirt while he squinted against the rain. Large drops soaked his clothes, quickly making him appear even skinnier and smaller next to Marc.

The rain didn't seem to faze Marc a bit.

"The officer here was just concerned I got hurt inside," Heather said quickly, feeling her makeup begin to run as rain fell harder by the minute.

"The officer?" Marc put his hands on his hips, looking like he might throw her over his shoulder, or across the street, she wasn't sure which.

Heather wiped rain from her eyes, realizing she'd offended him by implying they didn't know each other. Well hell!

"Heather. I'm getting soaked. Are we going to nab this story, or what?" Joey gave Marc a sideways glance as he spoke through his teeth. He nodded toward the building, his expression pleading with her to come on.

Marc's phone buzzed on his waist. Heather looked up into the hardened glare that he had fixed on her. Soaking wet, he still looked damned good.

"Looks like we both have jobs to do," she said, knowing if he didn't understand, then he wasn't meant for her.

What was she thinking? Did she seriously think she could make a go of having a relationship with a werewolf?

* * * * *

Marc accepted the fact that the force used him to handle the work the humans weren't capable of doing. He was stronger, faster, more capable of tracking than any other man on the force. He also accepted the fact that his pack relied on him for much of the same kind of work.

So when Rousseau called him later that evening, he figured the pack needed assistance with something, and agreed to come out without question. Not to mention he needed to get out of his den. He'd been pacing ever since he got home, outraged with Heather's denial of knowing him, and had been about ready to do exactly what he told himself he wouldn't do, and head over to her place.

Instead he decided a run through the backwoods to the pack leader's den would do him some good. He undid the cloth bag he'd tied around his neck when he resumed his human form in the yard behind Rousseau's home. Dressing without ceremony, he sniffed the place out, aware of more than several werewolves inside the small home.

Rousseau's mate answered the door, her cub in her arms. She stood to the side, letting him in with a friendly nod. Several *lunewulfs* sat at the kitchen table, within view of the front door.

"There you are, McAllister. Come on in." Johann Rousseau gestured with his hand.

Marc nodded to the men at the table. He knew all of them, and sensed the tension in the air. As he suspected, his help was needed for something. He waited to see what it was.

Instead of filling him in, Rousseau began talking about the events at City Hall earlier that day. Somehow Marc didn't think this was why he'd been called over, but he listened while the werewolves around the table expressed their concerns.

"The humans are right. Our cubs don't interact with their children. And we've never put them in their schools before."

"We can't just build a school, or even home-school them, without the proper permits from Prince George. Times aren't like they used to be." Johann stated what they all already knew.

"Well, I've got the lumber ready to go. I don't need a damned permit to build a building on my own land." Terry Roth was an older *lunewulf*, and known to be set in his ways.

Marc knew firsthand the werewolf didn't think he needed a permit to brew his own wine and sell it on his land, either.

"We've home-schooled our pups for years," the other *lunewulf* at the table said. "The humans are just making our lives hell, and they're doing it on purpose, you know that, don't you?"

The phone rang, and Rousseau's mate picked a cordless up from the counter.

"Johann, there's a situation going on down at Howley's." She adjusted her cub, who was the spitting image of his father, on her hip when the infant reached for the phone. "Apparently some of the human college kids and some of our pack are in a fight."

"Shit." Johann stood quickly, hurrying toward the front door. "We'll resume this conversation later," he yelled over his shoulder.

Marc was on his heels. They were out the front door before Johann turned on him.

"If you're going with me, then be sure you know where your loyalties lie."

Marc stopped in his tracks, Rousseau's words not making any sense. He could tell the werewolf's defenses were up though, and straightened.

"My loyalties shouldn't be in question," he said, his tone lowering.

"Word has it you have been seen with a human. You're too much in the public eye and right now I recommend you leave Miss Heather Graham alone."

It didn't surprise him that his pack leader knew he'd been with Heather. What details the werewolf may or may not have really didn't matter. One thing Marc knew beyond a doubt was that, pack leader or not, no one controlled who he spent time with.

Marc looked down at the *lunewulf*. "No one tells me who I will see or not see. Not even you."

For a *lunewulf*, Marc had to admit that Rousseau had guts. Johann took a quick step forward, jabbing his finger into Marc's chest. Marc didn't budge.

"You'll do as I fucking say, or you'll find yourself unemployed, and without a pack." Instantly Johann's teeth extended, anger filling the air around them. "Is that clear?"

Marc grabbed Rousseau's shirt, ready to tell him just how clear the matter was. The others flooded out of the door at that moment, Samantha Rousseau, with cub still in hand, dashing toward them. She almost jumped in between them.

"You two quit acting like cubs right now," she yelled.

Marc shoved Rousseau backwards, anger making his own vision more acute. He smelled the outrage on Rousseau's mate, and looked down at the petite bitch as she glared at the two of them.

"Both of you are better than this, and the day you let humans cause the two of you to fight will be the day *both* of you are looking for a new pack."

Hair prickled over the back of Marc's neck. Blood pumped hard through his veins, the change aching to take over, set his emotions free. The carnal side of him could much easier settle this matter. He remained focused on Johann, ignoring his mate.

"We can't reverse time. Humans know about us, and that won't change. I'll work by your side, or on my own. But my personal life is just that." His teeth pressed against his mouth, making his words a bit more garbled.

As desperately as he'd like to settle this matter physically, Marc would honor Johann's rank. But he wouldn't ignore Heather—he couldn't ignore her. Not for anyone.

"Now isn't the time." Johann recovered quickly from being shoved, moving closer slowly.

He wasn't intimidated by Marc's size or his strength. Anger burned in his eyes and his hardened expression. But he managed a cool tone, keeping his feelings at bay well enough so that their smells didn't permeate the air around them. His skills at controlling his inner beast were commendable.

"This pack has controlled this territory for over a hundred years. We date back to the founding of Fort Saint James. And with the awareness of werewolves around them now, we are on some damn shaky ground with humans. More so than ever before." Johann's patient tone grated on Marc's nerves.

"I don't need a fucking history lesson," he growled, managing to calm the beast in him enough that the darkness around him once again grew, his senses maintaining their human form. "We've got a situation down at Howley's. If you'd like my assistance, I'm there for you. If not, I'm going home."

Johann took a moment, staring at him. The others around them remained quiet, which was a damned good thing. Marc held Johann's gaze, allowing the werewolf time to accept his offer, or decline.

"I can handle the matter." Johann turned, without another word, and headed toward his Suburban.

Marc knew declining his offer meant his pack leader was upset with him. Well, so fucking be it. The *lunewulf* was out of line to tell him how to lead his own life. He took off around the side of the house, stripping once he was alone.

The change burned through him, anger and frustration egging it on. His body contorted, his heart pounding faster than a human body could handle. Feeling the cold night air against his fur, and inhaling the rich scents of the night, he burst into a hard run, needing to burn off energy.

It wasn't right for his pack leader to tell him who he could associate with. Werewolves had been interacting with humans for centuries, and peacefully too. Granted, now that the humans knew who they were, times had grown tougher. Yet that was exactly what had brought him together with Heather.

He hadn't voiced any commitment toward her. And at this point, he wasn't sure what type of relationship they had.

What he did know was that she was on his mind a lot—a hell of a lot more than any bitch he'd ever seen before.

Tearing across the countryside, pushing himself hard as he worked his way toward his house, he realized that was where his anger toward Rousseau had stemmed from. It bothered him that Heather had gotten under his skin. He'd wanted to show her how werewolves really were, and her saucy attitude and damn sex appeal had sent him for a spin.

Rousseau had been right. The timing on all of this sucked. And no matter how personal he would like to keep that side of his life, both he and Heather had high profile jobs. It wouldn't be possible.

And as bad as it had been for him just now with his pack leader, Marc knew it would be even worse for Heather if her kind were to find out.

He slowed his pace, suddenly not in a hurry to get anywhere. Quite possibly the best thing to do would be to leave her alone.

Chapter Nine

80

Heather took a deep breath before raising her hand to knock on Johann Rousseau's door. After she'd managed to get his phone number, it had taken over a day before she had the nerve to call him. Part of her just wanted to forget she'd ever wanted to write an article about werewolves.

But she needed to stay focused on her goals. Marc hadn't come around. If she didn't find something to concentrate on, she would go nuts. If only studying werewolves didn't make her think about him even more.

The tension between humans and werewolves in Prince George seemed to be escalating daily. Timing was perfect to put out a full-length article giving detailed insight on how these creatures lived. It would be the breaking point for her career, what she'd lived for, an answer to her dreams.

Yet every time she went on an assignment, showed up at a place where she knew werewolves were, she immediately found herself looking for Marc.

Tapping on the Rousseaus' door, she cursed herself silently for wondering if she might not see him while she was here. But that wasn't her reason for visiting with the pack leader. Somehow she needed to get Marc McAllister off of her brain.

"You must be Heather." A very pretty blonde answered the door, her hair short in a sporty punk haircut, and with just a touch of makeup. She even smelled good. "Come on in. I'm Samantha."

"It's nice to meet you. And thank you for letting me come over." Heather fought to hide her nervousness, wishing she didn't know how these werewolves could smell her emotions.

"I admit you have me a bit curious." Samantha shut the door behind Heather.

The Rousseau home was small but cozy-looking. Nothing near as fancy as Marc's home, yet Heather got the feeling there was a lot of happiness in this home. After a quick glance at the living room, and what she could see of a kitchen, she turned her attention to the pretty werewolf.

"Curious about what?"

"You told my mate you wanted to write an article about how werewolves lived, how we really are. I'm curious what you'll have to say, and why you're doing the article."

Johann walked down the hallway, joining them at that moment with an infant at his shoulder. Samantha turned, smiling warmly at him and the baby, and then went to take the child—cub.

Heather cocked her head, suddenly wishing she'd brought Joey so he could take pictures, when she noticed a long white tail hanging out of the infant's diaper. Otherwise, the baby looked human.

"Cubs have a hard time remaining in one form often until they are about three or four years old," Samantha told her quietly.

Heather nodded slowly. "That makes sense. I never thought about that before."

"It's kind of like potty-training. Human babies take a while to master that." Samantha nestled the infant to her breast. "Of course, so do werewolf babies," she added with a smile.

Suddenly Heather felt foolish. She'd wanted a camera to capture this child, like he was a freak or something. Yet his tail appearing hanging down his leg was a very natural thing. The only difference here was that he was a werewolf.

"Something just occurred to me," she said, looking from Samantha to Johann. "Werewolves know so much about humans. You've always known we were here. I want to write this article so that I can show my people the truth about you."

"And what is that truth?" Johann spoke for the first time, his tone guarded.

"That you aren't monsters." And what she didn't add was that would mean deleting every word she'd written so far.

But suddenly that was exactly what she wanted to do.

"I'd be interested in reading that article," Johann said, moving to the couch and gesturing for her to sit down.

"I promise you that I'll let you read what I write before it goes to print."

"So what's moved you to enlighten humans about us?" Johann asked, reclining on the couch and watching his mate.

"At first, I thought it would be the boost my career needed. We're at odds with each other, and I knew plastering a full-page spread about werewolves, with inside knowledge, would quite possibly get me national attention."

She knew her words weighed heavy with the two of them, and didn't realize she held her breath until her lungs suddenly hurt.

"At first?" Johann wasn't smiling when he gave her his full attention.

Heather nodded, hoping if she was completely open with these two that they would be apt to share more with her.

"Yes. At first." She bit her lip, going out on a limb here. But there was no stopping it. There was no way she could get into this interview until she'd said her piece. "I shared what I'd written with someone in your pack, and it outraged them. They told me it was trash and offered to show me how werewolves really were." Looking down, it seemed suddenly silly to confess this to them.

"Go on," Johann told her.

The way he said it made her feel she was confessing something to them. And maybe she was. Although she hadn't seen Marc lately, he still wouldn't stay out of her thoughts. And she couldn't keep this in her any longer. It wasn't like she could discuss this with any of her human friends.

"You've got a culture that I'd very much like to learn more about. And I think sharing what I learn with others like me might help to bridge the gap that exists between us right now." She looked up at Johann, his expression not readable. "I want to show the member of your pack who read my article that I can do better, that it won't be trash."

"You're talking about Marc McAllister," Samantha said.

"Samantha." Johann said her name so firmly that Heather jumped.

Immediately she noticed tension fill the air. Hell, she didn't have to be a werewolf to sense the emotions that flew between the two. It grew thick enough to cut with a knife.

"Yes. I am." She looked from one of them to the other, not understanding the silent communication they seemed to be relaying. "Is everything okay with him?"

Johann's attention snapped to her. "When's the last time you saw him?"

Heather shook her head. "Not for several days. Obviously I've upset him. This article has to help both of us — humans and werewolves. Will you give me the chance to try and do that?"

Samantha moved to sit next to Johann, and ran her hand over his arm. He seemed to noticeably relax, and she ached to ask more about Marc. That wasn't the reason she was here, she told herself. What she had just said to both of them she meant. She chewed on her lower lip, forcing herself to remain focused on what she knew she could do damned well if given the chance.

"You're taking on one hell of a battle," Johann said, relaxing into the couch and putting his arm around Samantha, with their werewolf baby in her arms. "But I commend you for it. Ask your questions."

Heather let out a breath she didn't realize she was holding and reached into her bag for her notes and her recorder. She had no clue how she would pull it off, but somehow she would put a dent, at least, in the animosity that existed between humans and werewolves. She had to.

An hour and a half later, Heather clicked off her recorder and popped out the cassette. She sipped at the water they'd offered her, feeling she had more werewolf knowledge in her head than she'd ever expected possible. Everything from how packs worked, to the tight-knit culture werewolves had, to the personal history of these two sitting opposite her.

"You make being a werewolf sound so appealing." She sighed, thinking of her own estranged family.

Samantha smiled. "Humans are just different. But you have something to envy too. You aren't shunned for who you are."

Johann patted her knee and then got up, heading into the kitchen.

"And that's another thing. You know so much about humans, but we know hardly anything about you."

"Actually, that isn't true. Humans have written about werewolves for centuries. You've just chosen to believe us as myths."

Heather nodded, her mind swirling with everything she'd been told. "Well, as is the case with most stories passed down through history, the facts are distorted."

"Well, we don't howl at the moon, if that's what you mean," Samantha said, chuckling.

Her expression grew serious then, and she glanced toward the kitchen before returning her attention to Heather.

"I think you've earned this tonight. I'm going to allow you to go see Marc for a bit," she said, and then added, "If you'd like that."

Heather couldn't stop the blush that spread over her cheeks. She smiled. "I think I might do that."

"What?" Johann barged into the living room, his voice bellowing loud enough that the baby jumped in Samantha's arms.

"She is a female. And I am queen bitch." Samantha cuddled their son to her chest, and began rocking slowly.

"And she is not a werewolf, let alone a member of this pack." Johann lowered his tone, but looked very pissed off.

Heather gathered her things and stood quickly. So did Samantha.

"Go. With my blessing," she said to Heather.

Johann stormed down the hallway, slamming a door.

Heather licked her lips but Samantha came up to her and patted her arm. "I know you want to."

"Thank you," Heather whispered, and let herself out the door.

She didn't understand the animosity she'd witnessed right before she left the pack leader's house. For whatever reason, it seemed Johann didn't want her seeing Marc. But that made no sense.

It was no more than a five-minute drive on the highway before she reached Marc's house. She shut off the engine, staring at the dark house. It didn't look like anyone was here.

Her tennis shoes crunched against the gravel in the drive as she walked up to the house, and then climbed the porch stairs to knock on the door. She knocked again, her heart swelling uncomfortably when there was no response.

She had to see Marc. It became imperative that she tell him about her interview tonight, what she had learned, how she was going to rewrite her article. It would mean so much to him. She knew that. And she had to tell him.

Not a floorboard squeaked as she paced the length of it once. Knocking one more time, this time harder, she stared at the solid structure around her. So much like Marc, strong and unyielding. Her surroundings smelled and breathed Marc

McAllister. Just standing on the porch, she could feel him around her, imagine him touching her. The swelling ache in her heart quickly traveled to the rest of her body.

She had to see him.

Almost jumping off the porch, skipping the steps and hurrying through the dark yard, she gave little thought other than the fact that she had to find him.

She walked with purpose around the side of the house, wondering if maybe his clothes might be on the deck. If he'd gone for a run, by damned, she would sit and wait for him. Her mind grew obsessed with telling him about her evening. His expression would light up with pride when she told him she planned on rewriting the article.

Coming around the side of the house, she froze in her tracks.

There in the middle of the yard stood a werewolf, tall and powerful-looking. He dominated the night, his head held high, muscles protruding throughout his body. And almond-shaped, silver eyes pinned her in mid-pace, staring her down as if he were ready to leap at the intrusion.

And in the next moment, he did just that. Pouncing to life, his mouth opened, sharp fangs with severe pointed ends, grabbing her attention, scaring the living shit out of her. He sprang to life, moving so quickly there was no escaping his attack.

"Shit. No!" she screamed, her arms covering her face as she feebly attempted to avoid him hurting her.

Chapter Ten

&)

Marc heard his brothers barking behind him, yelling at him to stop, but he ignored them. He hadn't made it more than a minute in the past few days without thinking about Heather. No matter how he buried himself in work, ran until he dropped from exhaustion, she wouldn't stay out of his head.

And now, here she was. Just standing there. The overcast sky, the deep darkness of the night, didn't stop him from seeing her sweet petite figure, the unsureness that covered her expression, and she was no dream.

He would make damn sure of it. No matter the reason she was here. Heather was here, and he would make sure she remained.

Leaping through the air, he needed to grab her, have her, hold her before she got away. His mind focused on nothing else. Several days might as well have been years. And he'd died without her. Nothing else mattered right now other than ensuring that she didn't turn around and leave.

Don't jump on her. You'll hurt her.

His brothers' barking and growling didn't sway him.

Heather shrieked, her scream tearing through the night as she lifted her arms, covering her face.

He reached her shirt, grabbing it with his teeth, needing her more than he needed to breathe.

Again she cried out. "Marc! It's me. God. Don't hurt me."

Pain wrenched through him as he realized he needed to change. His muscles already contorted, bones popping while blood slowed through his veins with a treacherous effort.

Carnal instinct battled throughout him.

Make her mine.

"Heather," he managed to cry out, when Gabe leapt on him.

Stone was right behind him.

Heather darted away from them. For a second he thought she would run away, escape him before he could get his brothers off of him.

But Heather ran onto his back deck, grabbing the broom leaning next to his back door.

"Get off of him," she screamed, slicing the broom handle through the air like a deadly weapon.

She managed to crack the handle over Gabe's back before he managed to change.

"See if I ever try to protect you again," he muttered, ducking out of her way as he headed to the deck for his clothes.

"Oh, shit." Heather stood there, her arms stretched out holding the broom handle like it was some science fiction laser beam weapon.

Marc straightened, honored that she fought to protect him. Carefully he removed the broom from her hands and tossed it to the ground. Heather simply stood there for a minute, staring at the three of them.

She must have realized at that second that she was staring at three naked men because she diverted her gaze, looking down quickly.

"Are you okay?" Marc whispered, wrapping his arms around her, drowning in her scent.

His cock raged to life, filling with blood at just the smell of her.

"You're a dumb fuck to have leapt at her like that," Stone muttered, always the one to condemn everyone else. Like he'd never pulled a stupid stunt in his life. "Not even I would try to filet my piece of ass."

"That's enough," Marc barked, not caring that they'd just prevented him from hurting her. He wouldn't be berated.

But Heather twisted in his arms. "Where in the hell have you been?" she cried out, surprising him when she suddenly beat his chest with her fists. "You think you can just ignore me until the next time you want to fuck?"

Gabe snickered but Marc ignored both of his brothers.

"Heather." He grabbed her fists, pinning them as he pressed them against her breasts.

She looked up at him with fiery emerald eyes, her lips pursed together in anger.

"You're a good little boy to behave and stay away from me because you think I'm some nasty human."

Everything inside him hardened. The spicy smell of anger filled the air around them. Heather had a nasty temper when she was pissed. But he didn't miss the fact that she was obviously hurt that he'd stayed away.

"There are things you don't understand," he told her through clenched teeth.

"I understand that you honor your pack over me."

"Do you?" He almost lifted her when he turned her toward his deck, and then pushed her toward the back door.

It was getting damn cold out here now that he was in his skin.

Heather followed his brothers into his home. Neither had bothered turning on a light, but already Gabe was tossing a few logs into the fireplace.

"Samantha suggested that I come see you. So I guess I honor your pack, too."

Both of his brothers stopped what they were doing and looked at her. Heather simply stared at the three of them, obviously not understanding what the implication of the queen bitch's suggestion had meant.

Marc turned on the lamp in his living room, watching her as she looked from one of them to the other. If Samantha had told Heather to come over here, then it meant she approved of a mating. Of course, that would apply if Heather were a werewolf, which she wasn't. He wondered what Johann's reaction to his mate's suggestion was.

"When did you talk to Samantha?" Marc asked, smelling her sudden nervousness as she stared at his brothers.

He let his gaze follow her hands when she adjusted her coat, and then rubbed her hips as if trying to dry her palms.

Gabe returned to building a fire. Stone simply watched her, indifferent to the fact that he stood before her in boxers. Marc knew what was on his younger brother's mind. And he'd be damned if he would let his littermates put Heather ill at ease. He picked up his brother's jeans and tossed them at him. Stone glared at him but didn't say anything. He wouldn't dare. It was Marc's way of telling him that he had no intention of sharing.

"I just came from their house—from your pack leader's house. Johann let me interview them." Her entire expression lit up.

Obviously she was quite excited about her article—that damned article. Johann wasn't a fool though. The pack leader would have watched what he told Heather.

"And you told them that you're fucking our brother, so they said to please go over and take care of him?" Stone had never been good at tact. He let his gaze stroll down her, licking his lips hungrily.

Even in the dim light, Marc could see the pink blush spread over Heather's cheeks. He moved to her, stroking the warmth of her face. Then reaching under her coat, he slid it from her shoulders and then down her arms. She wasn't going anywhere anytime soon.

"That's enough, Stone," he growled, giving his brother a threatening glare as he took Heather's coat over to the closet.

"No. That isn't what was said." Heather's tone turned defiant.

He would enjoy watching her take his brothers down a few notches.

"Forgive my brother." Gabe smiled at her, his winning smile that had won the twins so many bitches in the past. "He doesn't think with the head on his shoulders."

"I thought that was just a human trait in men," she snapped.

Marc fought a grin, wondering if she knew how she'd just insulted Stone.

"The way I understand it, we all have dicks." Stone wasn't daunted. He looked at Marc. "So, are you going to share her?"

Gabe smacked his brother on the side of the head. Marc simply shook his head, already seeing that Heather was more skittish than some of the deer they'd tracked on their runs.

"Actually, you were just leaving," Marc informed him, his tone warning enough to have his brothers grabbing the rest of their clothes.

Gabe and Stone had never kept it a secret that they often shared their bitches, enjoying swapping places and seeing if the female could tell which one of them was which. If a female didn't know the twins well, they wouldn't notice the only difference in them being Gabe's hint of strawberry blonde hair, a trait he'd inherited from their sire. But Heather wasn't ready for anything like that. He didn't have to ask her to know. Her unease with his younger littermates' comments filled the room with its awkward smell.

Not to mention, he wasn't sure he wanted to share her.

Heather crossed her arms over her chest, watching as the twins carried their clothes out to the deck. Marc followed them to the doorway while they stripped out of their boxers and wrapped their clothes in sacks they would tie to their necks.

Gabe and Stone dropped to all fours as the change consumed them, then darted off the deck into the night.

"You didn't have to chase them away on my account," Heather said behind his back. He turned to see she'd turned her attention to the fire. "Why is he called Stone? Is that a family name, or something?"

Marc laughed. "No," he said, shaking his head. "When he was a cub he always banged his head into everything and it never fazed him. So our mother said he had a head of stone. The name just stuck. His name is Frederic."

Heather nodded while nervousness suddenly filled the air. She hesitated before glancing sideways at him.

"They are both good men." He watched her, noting her conservative attire that she'd obviously donned to go over to the pack leader's house. But even in jeans and a pullover sweater, she was hot as fucking hell. "If you noticed, they were ready to fight to protect you when I lunged at you."

Heather shivered. "And why did you do that?"

He cupped her chin, feeling her pulse beat heavily against his finger when he held her face in his hand. "I think differently in my fur and will take what I feel is mine."

She swallowed heavily, looking up at him, her green eyes darkening as she stared.

"Do you know..." he began, stroking her silky strawberry-blonde hair away from her face, holding her so that she couldn't look away, "when a queen bitch sends a female to a werewolf's den, she is stating that she approves of the mating."

He gave her a moment, her eyes wide and glowing in the dim light while the fire made her hair seem to glow around her flushed expression. She made an effort to turn, but he couldn't let her go. Instead he wrapped his arms around her, pulling her to him.

"I'm not a werewolf," she whispered, moistening her lips as her gaze fell to his mouth.

He nibbled on her lower lip, then tasted her sweet mouth before tightening his grip and kissing her thoroughly.

No. She wasn't a werewolf. But damn it to hell if she didn't make him crazy in the head when he was around her. She had the fire of a beautiful bitch, sexy and aggressive, yet with a tendency to be shy enough to make his blood boil.

Needing to touch her flesh, he shoved her sweater up, and ran his hands over her breasts, the cool material of her bra almost as enticing as how her nipples hardened into eager pebbles.

She let out a sigh, opening to him, tasting him in return as their tongues began a slow, sultry dance. Heather was like a cat in heat, stretching against him, her hands strolling up his arms until she wrapped them around his neck.

Suddenly all that mattered was that he get her out of her clothes. Breaking the kiss, hearing her gasp for air, he tugged at her sweater while a fever raced through him. His mind burned with need. Fire raced through his veins. Blood pumped through him so hard that his muscles ached to grow, make room for the raw cravings that consumed him.

"Marc," she cried out, when he yanked her sweater from her, tossing it to the side and then reached for her bra.

Her heavy breathing as she looked at him, with her hair tousled, her eyes wide with burning lust, hardened every muscle inside him. He grabbed her bra between her breasts and tore it from her.

"Oh shit," she said, taking a step backwards.

He didn't smell fear, but instead he almost drowned in her rich sweet scent of need. Need for him.

Her fingers darted over her bare skin, while she licked her lips and stared up at him. "You aren't going to hurt me," she said, not asking, but more like reminding him.

"Tell me no, and I'll stop," he told her.

And then reached for her again. She didn't protest when he dragged her to him, grabbing her jeans and popping the top button off. He almost ripped her zipper from the fabric, forcing it down, peeling them off her legs. Again, he tossed the clothing to the side.

Heather almost stumbled, reaching to stabilize herself. But he needed her down, had to have her now. She collapsed to the floor and he came down on top of her. She rolled over quickly, spreading her legs, offering her pussy to him.

And he took what he was offered.

Heather felt the carpet scrape against her back when Marc grabbed her legs, sliding her to him, lifting her ass off the floor. Kneeling before her, he brought her pussy to his mouth.

Dear Lord.

"Marc. You're wild." She gripped his hair, closing her eyes when he sank his tongue between her moist folds.

"*Cariboo lunewulf* tend to get that way," he whispered, his breath as torturous as his tongue.

Her inner thigh muscles stretched, his large hands pressing firmly against her skin, holding her spread wide-open so he could feast upon her. And good God, he was a starving man. She would faint, absolutely pass out and miss the most pleasurable experience ever offered her.

Glancing up through blurred vision, she took in Marc's broad shoulders, the intent look on his face while his eyes seemed to roll back in his head. His tongue stroked and teased her, built a pressure inside her that would explode out of her control.

She fought to bring her legs together, ease away from him just a bit so the intensity wouldn't grow so quickly. His tongue glided in and out of her, then circled over her swollen clit, driving her nuts. And he wouldn't let her move her legs. He kept her pinned, not allowing her to move other than to thrust her pussy up against his face.

And when she did that he growled, opening his eyes to stare at her. Blue mixed with silver—what erotic eyes he had.

"I can't take it," she cried out, fisting her hands and pounding the floor next to him.

She tried to grab him but couldn't raise her shoulders off the ground far enough with her ass already in the air. And he didn't let up. His lips suckled on her clit, torturing the most sensitive part of her body, making her entire body tense.

"You can take it," he murmured, his voice sending shivers rushing through her.

"No. You're killing me." She thrashed her head from side to side.

The pressure inside her would explode, taking her with it. She wouldn't recover. There was no way she could endure this another minute.

Yet he showed no mercy, continuing to fuck her with his tongue and then scrape his teeth and lips over her cunt, devouring her.

When she began trembling, he let up, suddenly barely touching her. Her orgasm reached its head, ready to spill out of her, brimming over and threatening her sanity, when he lifted his head.

"Damn you," she yelled, thrusting her hips up toward his face as hard as she could.

Marc chuckled, sounding absolutely fucking demonic, as he brought her ass to the floor, leaving her on the edge of the hardest orgasm she knew she ever had experienced. Except she didn't get to experience it.

The second he let go of her thighs she came at him with her fists, intent on pounding his chest, pushing him back, and getting at his cock so she could ride out the orgasm that threatened to well over.

Marc grabbed her wrists, pulling her to him. Tempering his strength, knowing even with his brain burning with fiery lust that he didn't want to hurt her, he brought her to her knees, and then held her there.

"Now my little bitch, it's your turn," he whispered, his tone so serious she forgot to reprimand him for calling her that.

"You just deprived me of my turn," she pouted.

"You're right where I want you," he said. "Now I want to see how good you are at sucking my cock."

Heather remembered the last time she'd done this. In college, with a guy she'd dated a while in her psych class. His name was Ted Bullings, and after about six months their class schedule had changed and they had drifted apart. But she remembered the night she'd offered to give him head. He'd grinned from ear to ear, agreeing enthusiastically. After just a few minutes, he'd exploded all over her face. And then he'd been done, leaving her horny.

There was no comparison between Marc McAllister and Ted Bullings though.

She knelt before him, unable to say a word as she stared at his muscular body and rock-hard cock. Her pussy convulsed in anticipation at the sight of him. Licking her lips, her mouth suddenly too damned wet, she watched his long fingers stroke that powerful-looking cock.

There couldn't possibly be an ounce of fat anywhere on the man. And in the glow of the fire behind her, muscles appeared to ripple underneath his skin. She reached out, stroking her fingernails over his thighs, and then spread her hands over his abdomen.

His cock thrust toward her face.

"Suck it for me." His voice was raspy.

She glanced up at him.

"Don't you dare come." Her body was on edge, tense and in need. She wouldn't be left out again.

He smiled, and gripped her head, his large hands tangling in her hair while she opened her mouth, running her tongue over the swollen tip of his cock head.

Marc growled, tightening his hold on her.

She wrapped her fingers around his thick shaft, feeling it pulse with life. Sucking him into her mouth, she began slowly taking him in, his thickness and length making it impossible to take more than half of him.

But she'd been aching for him—craving him was more like it. And now that she was here, giving him this pleasure, it made her tingle with an energy she hadn't experienced before. More than anything she wanted Marc to feel the same satisfaction that he'd just given her. Damn good oral sex. Although if he came before she did, somehow she'd figure out a way to kick his ass.

"Your mouth is so fucking hot." He held her head so tight that she couldn't move.

Slowly he began fucking her face, moving in and out of her mouth while her lips curved around him. She lapped at him, learning his salty taste, enjoying it as he swelled in her mouth.

"That's it, little bitch. Wrap your mouth around my cock." He ran his hands over her head, allowing her a bit of freedom to take on his cock.

Moving in close, she buried her face in his crotch, running her hands up his powerful torso as she devoured him, all thought of him coming dissipating as she stroked his cock with her mouth.

"You are so fucking good," he growled, his body hardening under her touch.

His muscles were quivering, growing and bulging. She wondered if she pushed him to the point where he would lose control of his ability to remain human.

There were so many things to learn about this man, what made him tick, what pushed him to the edge, how to control him.

Marc growled, his body convulsing under her touch, while his cock filled her mouth, salty and so damned hard. Her pussy throbbed in response. She needed him so damned bad.

Releasing him, she moved before he could grab her head. It took a little effort to stand, her legs suddenly feeling like jelly. But she wouldn't let him see any sign of weakness.

"Sit down," she ordered, loving the glazed look on his face.

A powerful giant, he stared down at her for a moment as if not understanding, and she pushed against his chest, knowing damned good and well she wouldn't be able to budge him an inch if he didn't want to move.

"Think you're in charge, do you?" A slow smile appeared on his face when he backed up the few feet to his couch.

He reclined, taking her hand when she moved to straddle him.

"Someone's got to be," she whispered, grabbing his blond hair the way he had grabbed hers, and pulling his head back. "Now give me what I want."

"You like playing with fire?" He grabbed her hips and then thrust deep inside her.

Heather swore he impaled her clear up to her throat.

"Holy shit!" Her hands slipped to his shoulders before she could stop herself.

Marc gripped her firmly, holding her in place as he fucked the shit out of her.

All she could do was hold on and pray she didn't fall off the couch while she exploded so hard she could feel the moisture trail down her inner thighs. She soaked his balls that slapped against her while he continued to move, showing her no mercy. Never in her life had she been fucked so hard, and loved it so damn much.

"Don't stop," she managed to cry out, as she felt another wave of passion rip through her.

"Little bitch. You will learn who gives the orders around here."

"Just fuck me."

He slowed, but this time her orgasm was too close. Exploding once again, she collapsed against his chest, her entire body on fire.

His cock was so large, caressing her deep inside with slow, fluid motions. But then he seemed to grow larger, throbbing while he stretched her soaked muscles.

Lifting her head, she blinked to clear her vision and tried to ride him. His expression hardened, muscles twitching in his jaw while he ground his teeth together and stared at her with almost silver eyes. For a moment she could see the werewolf in the man.

"Don't move." He spoke through a clenched jaw.

His hips barely moved, his motions shaky as he swelled further in her and then let out a low growl that started deep in his chest and rumbled through him until he threw his head back and howled. His cock seemed to explode inside her, filling her, consuming her while his body shook with the intensity of his own orgasm.

Heather wasn't sure she could have moved if she wanted to.

"Are you okay?" she whispered, when he'd quit moving yet his cock seemed to still be incredibly hard and impaling her to the point where she wasn't sure she could pull herself off of him.

His head had fallen back on the couch, and he ran his hands up her back, encouraging her to lie against him.

"Never been better," he murmured. "You brought out the beast in me, Heather."

His heart pounded with a solid steady beat above her breast. Hard and solid, the warmth of his body encased her, while his cock continued to throb, calming slowly, inside her.

"I'm not sure the beast has ever left you," she said, smiling as she cuddled into him. "And I doubt you would be the same if it did."

Feeling the stretch in her thighs, she tried to adjust herself but his cock remained firmly impaled. It was as if she were stuck on him.

"Well, this time you did a damn good job. It will take a few minutes before I can slide out of you."

She raised her head, and he stroked the hair from her face.

"Do you mean like a dog?"

"I mean like a werewolf."

"You wouldn't ever change while we were having sex, would you?"

Marc shook his head. "No. But even in my human form I'm different than you are. And for the moment, we're bound together. We've truly mated."

Truly mated? But mating for werewolves was a stronger bond than marriage was for humans. Werewolves didn't get divorced. In all of her research she'd found that especially appealing about this race of creatures. Their tight bond to their pack, their den, was enviable. But how could she have mated with Marc? She was human for crying out loud. Their rules didn't apply to her.

Heather chuckled. There was so much she still needed to learn about his kind. "Well, it was good for me, too."

She relaxed into him again, realizing she could stay like this forever and it wouldn't be long enough. Her pussy felt more stretched than she thought possible, and the heat between them made her insides throb. But it felt damned good. Her eyes grew heavy, and she relaxed further, enjoying his arms securely wrapped around her.

Chapter Eleven

ഌ

Marc woke up ravenous, and would normally have crawled out of bed to find something to eat, or enjoy an early morning run and capture his kill for breakfast.

Heather lay next to him though. Once his cock had finally relaxed the night before, she'd been contentedly sleeping on his chest. He'd carried her to his bed, wanting nothing more than to sleep with her.

Waking up with her next to him felt perfect.

She hadn't understood what he'd told her the night before. If she were a werewolf they would be mated—mated for life.

The pack leader knew she was here. It wouldn't surprise him at all if Rousseau did a drive-by, or had his mate drive by to see if she'd left yet. They would see her car parked at his den, know what had happened. And if circumstances were different, when Heather woke they would make a trip to the pack leader, announcing their mating. And then she would be his.

But that wasn't how it was.

Marc rolled over, staring at her while she slept, and gently brushed a strand of hair that had fallen over her eye.

Her lashes fluttered, and she murmured something then buried herself deeper under his covers. He wrapped a leg over her, pulling her next to him.

There were matters to discuss, things to figure out. But he would feed her, give her time to wake up as he tried to think things through in his head.

Never in his life had he considered the thought that he would take a human as a mate. He wasn't sure even if it had ever been done before.

Heather moved against him, stirring his cock to life. He didn't move, knowing the chances of her being pretty sore this morning were good. She'd been so fucking hot the night before she'd managed to make him lock inside of her. No werewolf bitch had ever managed to get him to do that before.

His father's words, told to the three of them when they were teenagers, rang through his head.

"Lock inside a bitch and she's yours. That's the true sign, boys."

Did that apply to humans?

"Good morning." Heather's voice sounded sleepy, raspy.

Her face was nestled against his chest, barely visible under the covers. She didn't move.

"It's a damned good morning so far."

He could feel her smile against him.

"You shouldn't have let me sleep here though." She stretched, her breasts torturing him and the moisture between her legs leaving a trail against his thigh. "I should get out of here before anyone discovers that I did."

He tightened his grip. "No."

"What about your brothers? Or your pack leader?"

"It's the weekend. They'll all sleep in and it's early." Not that he gave a rat's ass about any of them. "My brothers wouldn't care if you were here anyway."

She moved against him, slowly pulling herself to a sitting position. He didn't want her out of his arms but allowed her to move. She ran her hand over her chest, not meeting his gaze.

"Do all werewolves share their women?"

Her question shouldn't have surprised him. Gabe and Stone weren't too shy about their sexual behaviors. And he should have expected the question.

Heather licked her lips, a slow blush creeping over her face. That and the way her hair tousled adorably around her face made him ache to pull her over him.

"I mean," she added quickly. "I know you had this law about having more than one mate."

"That law doesn't exist anymore. The previous pack leader created it in order to keep the *lunewulf* breed strong. But it caused a lot of jealousy from what I hear, and was abolished. That was before I joined this pack though. And no, not all werewolves share their bitches."

Heather nodded, and then crawled to the edge of his bed, climbing out of it and then padding naked to his bathroom.

When he heard his shower start, he decided to join her.

Her head was under the showerhead when he stepped into his shower. Already she'd lathered her hair, and soapy water created trails down her body. All he could do was stand and enjoy the view for a moment.

Reaching for his soap, he lathered it up in his hands, and then reached for her breasts.

Heather jumped. "You could have told me you were in here," she said, sputtering water as she quickly wiped her eyes.

Her nipples were so hard they made his mouth water. And for such a tiny woman, they were good-sized, perfect for sucking and nibbling. His cock danced to life as he wrapped his arm around her, cradling her while she stood.

"Are you tender?" he asked, putting the soap down and running his hand down her belly toward her shaved cunt.

"Just a little." She sighed when he parted her folds, gently stroking her.

For such a petite woman—hell, her feet were half the size of his—she had an aura about her that made her seem larger than life.

"Why did your brother ask if you were going to share me?" she asked.

Her eyelashes dripped with water, making her green eyes wide and clear as a deep pond. He wouldn't fuck her again so soon, although his cock was hard as nails at the moment. It would take breaking her in before she could handle what he offered on a very regular basis.

Turning her around, he took the soap to her back, taking his time in answering the question that he felt she'd already guessed the answer to.

"They like what they see." There was no reason to offer too much information.

"You've shared women with them in the past?"

He should have guessed the reporter in her wouldn't let the matter die.

"Once or twice."

She let him bathe her, and then took the soap from him and washed him thoroughly, keeping her head down, and focusing intently on his cock while she stroked it with her soapy hands.

"You better be able to finish what you start," he growled, the pressure building while her soft little hands created a heat he ached to put out deep inside her.

"Did you share women you were dating? Or were they just one-night stands?" she asked, focusing on his cock while she pressed and pulled, building up the lather around his shaft.

He braced against the side of the shower, the steam filling the room growing heavy with the smell of lust.

"You'd have to ask Stone and Gabe. They were their women." If she thought she could manipulate answers out of him while stroking his cock, she would learn he had a hell of a lot more control than that. "Why? Are you interested in fucking them too?"

She moved her head enough to allow the shower to rinse his cock. He gripped her head when she looked like she would stand.

"No. I'm just interested in knowing all there is to know about you." With the soap gone, she once again began stroking his cock, watching her efforts.

He pulled her head closer to his cock. "You're taking that in your mouth, or your pussy. You choose."

"You think you can boss me around?" she asked, looking up at him with defiant green eyes. "Because I choose neither."

A growl escaped him, her challenging him when he could so easily force her to do either, or both, calling the more carnal side of him forward. She knew damned good and well he would never hurt her or, for that matter, make her do anything she didn't want to do. Muscles bulged and hardened throughout him when she grinned up at him.

"Come for me, darlin'," she whispered, her tone turning seductive as she knelt before him with the water streaming over her naked body. "I want to watch you come. Will you do that?"

This woman was half his size. She was petite, probably had never been in a fight in her life. He could easily lift her with one hand, and do with her as he pleased. Yet she knelt before him, trying to tell him how it would be.

Damn it all to living hell.

"If I jack off for you," he told her through gritted teeth, "then you will come for me. You will do it when I say, and how I say to do that. Do we have a deal?"

She looked up at him, her hands not relenting as she continued to stroke his shaft, torture him slowly and thoroughly. Her eyes were moist as she ran her tongue over her damp lips. Even with her hair wet and clinging to her head, she was the most beautiful creature he'd ever laid eyes on.

Her mouth parted, her answer right there, yet she hesitated. Marc could see clearly that she didn't like someone getting the upper hand with her. Well, if she wanted to be with him she would learn now that he didn't take orders easily.

"I'll think about it," she said finally, a small smile appearing as if content that he'd just found her out.

She lowered her head, brushing water from her face, and then watched with a smile on her face when he took his shaft in his hand and began stroking. When she reached between his legs and began tickling his balls, he thought he might explode right there. Letting his head fall back, he clamped his teeth together so hard it made his jaw hurt.

She focused so intently on his cock, watching with her head lowered so that he couldn't see her face. Her hands worked a cruel and torturous magic, stroking and caressing his inner thighs while he held his cock so that the blood boiled through his veins. The pressure built to a breaking point, and standing like this, maintaining his dignity and not grabbing her hair and forcing her mouth on his cock, became so much of a chore he couldn't think straight.

"Come for me," she cooed, her innocent tone defying the expertise of her hands.

"Little bitch," he rumbled, then grabbed her head, knocking her off balance when he thrust his cock in her face.

She regained her balance, adjusting herself under the flow of the shower, then gave him a wicked grin. "Now, now. Behave," she scolded.

He pulled her hair so hard she closed her eyes, although didn't tell him to stop. He'd give her enough intelligence to know that she was pushing him beyond his limits.

"Open your mouth." She would pay later for her torture session, he would see to it.

Right now, he would give her what she wanted.

The shower sprayed over her face when she looked up at him, her face right in front of his cock. She did as he said.

Opening her mouth, letting the water streak down her face while he looked down at her, she blinked the water out of her eyes while watching him.

Focusing, concentrating, using everything he had not to shove his cock down her throat, he exploded on her, watching as the white cream was caught in the water and rushed down her, over her tits.

God. What a sight.

Droplets of water clung to her eyelashes making her green eyes look even more like they were glowing. The shower streaked through his cum, rinsing it down her neck.

"It doesn't look any different."

"What did you expect?"

"Last night." She stood slowly, her hands still holding his shaft, while she looked up at him, her face flooding with curiosity. "You felt so different inside me. I wanted to see how you changed."

"And that is why you pulled this little stunt?" He frowned, realizing that her act had been more to learn than for sexual pleasure. That didn't ride well with him.

"I've seen you as a werewolf and as a human, but I wanted to see..."

Marc reached around her and turned off the water, then pulled back the shower curtain to grab a towel. "I don't perform tricks. You'll do well to remember that."

She didn't say anything, which was a damn good thing. Reaching for the other towel, she slowly began drying herself. He was aware that she watched him though.

Wrapping the towel around his waist, he turned to see the caution on her face. His little bitch definitely needed a lot of education.

"And remember, next time, you will perform for me."

Chapter Twelve

ജ

Heather knew there was no way she'd be able to concentrate with Marc's promise lingering over her.

Next time, you will perform for me.

It didn't help that she'd seen him three times that day. He'd shown up at the *Tribune*, there to answer questions for another reporter. The way his gaze locked onto hers captured her from across the room. She couldn't remember whether she was coming or going after that.

Then to make matters worse, during lunch downtown, she'd seen him again, driving by as she hurried to her car. He hadn't stopped. He didn't have to. The way he looked at her made her so damned wet, she almost stumbled in her heels, missing the curb.

"Damn him." He was controlling her with his simple promise of making her pay for what she'd done in the shower.

And all she'd wanted was to understand him better. The sex they'd had on his couch had been so different from anything she'd ever experienced. It had *felt* different. In no way would she claim to be an expert on sex. But he'd changed inside of her. And well, that had freaked her out.

All she'd wanted to do was see that change, understand it, and him, better.

Not to mention she ached to see him again, and had no idea when that would be.

By the end of the day, she just happened to take the route to her apartment that went past the police station. He pulled out of the parking lot as she drove by. It was hard to keep her attention from her mirrors when she realized he was right behind her. The light in front of her turned red, and she slammed on the brakes.

Her cell phone buzzed, and she expected to hear Marc's voice chastising her for not having her wits about her.

"You better spill it, Heather," her girlfriend Margot said teasingly when she answered her phone. "Who was that gorgeous man who practically hauled you out of the coffee shop?"

"His name is Marc McAllister. He's a cop." And a werewolf. But that was more information than she would allow.

Margot Mason was a good friend, and someone she'd met shortly after moving to Prince George. Margot worked in the distribution center at the newspaper, and was inclined to always be up on the latest gossip. Harmless enough, but Heather doubted something as juicy as "the up-and-coming reporter sleeping with a werewolf" would be information her friend would keep to herself.

"Well, he's an absolute hunk. Are you dating?"

Heather glanced at her rearview mirror, her mouth going dry when she saw Marc's determined expression. He wasn't more than a car length behind her. She turned the corner, watching as he continued to follow her.

"I'm not sure, to be honest with you." And she wasn't.

Technically, Marc hadn't asked her out on a date. Unless she wanted to count the night he'd informed her she was going to his brothers' party with him. Maybe that was how werewolves did dating.

Something told her Marc did things exactly how he wanted to do them, regardless of what werewolf protocol might be.

"Well, a bunch of us will be down at the bowling alley Wednesday night. You should bring him along. Let us all drool." Margot laughed easily. "You don't date enough as it is.

And this one, with that aggressive side. Sounds like you'd be a fool to pass him up."

Heather pulled into her parking lot and turned off her car. She stepped out as Marc pulled in next to her.

"I'll have to see," she said, distracted by how damn good he looked in his cop uniform.

"Heather." Margot sighed. "You bury yourself in your work and we all know it. Now if this man is interested in you, have some fun. You'll ask him, won't you?"

Heather almost chuckled. Have some fun? Marc had given her better sex than she'd ever dreamed possible. The man was wild, damn near uncontrollable, and sexier than any man she'd ever seen. Granted he borderlined on dangerous, but she couldn't deny the fact that that excited her.

Marc strolled up to her, taking a strand of her hair and wrapping it around his finger then giving it a tug. She let her head fall back, almost forgetting she was on the phone when she drowned in those powerful blue eyes.

Definitely dangerous.

"Apparently you made quite an impression on our pack leader." His deep tone turned her insides upside down.

Her palm grew damp against her phone and at the same time her pussy began throbbing. Just staring at him was enough to unnerve her. Her mind seemed to melt, all coherent thought seeping from her as her body began throbbing with lustful need.

"Who is that? Is he there with you? What did he say?" Margot's excited voice brought her back to reality.

"I just got home. And yes, he's here." Awkwardness plummeted through her.

It was impossible to talk to Margot with Marc this close to her. He smelled like soap, and so much man. Looking straight ahead her vision was filled with his massive chest. Glancing up, he devoured her with his hungry look.

"Ask him about the bowling alley. You've just got to bring him. Give us all a chance to get to know him."

"Okay. I'll ask him. Talk later, okay?"

She hung up her phone after hasty goodbyes and stuffed it in her purse.

"Ask me what?" he asked, as his gaze traveled down her body.

Even in her dark suit pants, complete with matching jacket, heat swarmed through her. No matter how chilly the late afternoon air was, it did nothing to stop the smoldering lust that pooled between her legs.

Heather waved her hand in the air, dismissing the conversation she'd just had on the phone. There was no way she could picture Marc hanging out with her girlfriends and their husbands. They were such a lame bunch compared to him and the pack members she'd met the other night. He would think her a total bore if he saw that side of her.

"Nothing," she said, straining her brain to think of something else to talk about.

She turned, grabbing her briefcase from her car, and then shut the door. Marc hadn't moved.

"So Johann Rousseau liked me?" she asked, unsure whether to start toward her apartment or stay put.

"I said you made quite an impression on him." The way he squinted against the setting sun brought out adorable crow's feet on either side of his eyes. "He seems to think you might be able to help gap the bridge between werewolves and humans."

"That's what I told him I was going to try and do."

"So you lied."

She stared at him for a moment, resenting instantly that he would think her incapable of completing such a feat.

"No. I didn't lie. That is exactly what I want to do." She ached to touch him, anything to take that hardened expression from his face.

All day she'd dreamed of more sex with him, spending time learning more about him. Hell, she'd even considered the idea of riding a dirt bike again while he ran as a werewolf. Now those awesome fantasies seemed to fade as she looked up at him.

"You forget, little bitch," he said, barely moving his mouth.

"I don't know why you have to keep calling me that," she interrupted.

"You forget that I've seen the article you're writing," he continued, ignoring her comment.

Cupping her chin, he stroked her jawbone slowly, gently, the action sending shivers through her as she fought to keep her breath steady.

"I've learned quite a bit since I started writing the article. Most of what you've read will be changed. I really want to see werewolves and humans get along. This article will help. You'll see."

The way he stroked her flesh, moving his finger from her jawbone, down the side of her neck, was such a slow, sultry motion it unnerved her. Slow and gentle hadn't been Marc's style from the moment she'd met him. The thought that he held her face and her neck, with the power to grip too hard and with no notice, steal her breath away, sent a rush of nervous excitement through her.

Marc's eyes were a hard, radiant blue. So damned controlled and powerful. "And why is it that you so desperately want us to get along?"

"That's a silly question."

She yanked her head away from him, unable to take the slow torturous caress any longer. Whatever it was that had gotten under his skin, she wasn't sure she liked it. Rubbing her neck quickly, she marched around him toward her apartment.

Heather would have to run to make him work to keep up with her. Marc moved alongside her with a determined gait, pausing when she reached her apartment door and fumbled for her keys.

Once in her small apartment, Marc closed the door behind them. With his powerful and large body in her living room, he made everything around him appear small.

She tossed her briefcase on her small dining room table, neatly arranged with placemats for two—placemats she seldom ever used. There was no reason to fix nice meals for just her.

Sitting on her couch, she kicked off her heels and rubbed her ankles through her hose. Marc reclined in her chair opposite the couch, stretching out his long legs, which almost reached her as he relaxed. His brooding expression made her nervous.

"You're just staring at me," she finally said, unable to take his watchful gaze a moment longer. "It's making me nuts."

Marc lifted a shoulder lazily, his expression not changing. "Oftentimes that is an emotion of a guilty party."

"I'm not guilty of anything." He was starting to make her mad.

Which was so damned unfair. All day long she'd fantasized about this man. She had no idea what had crawled up his ass, but she didn't like it.

"Why are you writing the article?" he asked again, his baritone sending chills rushing over her.

It would be a damned good idea never to be interrogated by this man. She wouldn't stand a chance.

The best approach was honesty. After all, she had nothing to hide. Straightening, she gripped her knees.

"Originally I thought the timing was perfect. Writing an informative and accurate article about werewolves would do wonders for my career. We're dying to know more about you. We know you exist, yet you're a mystery. And no one has dug deep into your culture yet and informed the world of how you really are." She took a breath, hating how his expression didn't change. His posture remained the same. It was as if he was made of stone, not breathing, not moving, simply staring at her. She pressed on. "I thought if I could get inside your pack, learn how you live, learn everything about you, then I would be able to write the best damn article that would give me worldwide attention."

Marc pounced at her, moving so quickly she didn't have a chance to catch her breath before he grabbed her, lifting her off of the couch.

Her feet left the ground. He gripped her arms, giving her a quick shake that rattled her teeth.

"I will not be used," he growled with enough fierceness that she should've been terrified.

Instead she was outraged. Twisting in his grip, her feet hit the floor hard when he let go of her. She reached for the first thing she could find — her briefcase. Hurling it at him, he grabbed it all too easily and tossed it on the chair where he'd just been sitting.

"I'm not using you." She had enough sense not to scream, knowing her not so thick walls would have all the neighbors turning down their televisions to listen if she started yelling. "Aren't you the one who can smell emotions? You know damn good and well I'm not using you."

"You're interviewing the pack leader, befriending his mate. And then you want me to perform for you, masturbating so you can watch and see if you can change me." Silver streaks appeared in his eyes, while his jaw twitched as he spoke. "You may not see it, Heather, but I see it plain as day. That article depicts us as monsters. That won't do a thing to bring humans and werewolves together."

Heather grabbed his arm, attempting to pull him into her bedroom where her laptop was. Marc didn't budge.

"Come here." She looked up at his hardened face, lines creasing around his mouth and eyes as he stared, not blinking, down at her. "I want to show you something. Now move."

A growl burst through him, and he grew larger before her eyes. Her heart raced, but she didn't fear him. Although her heart swelled to the point where she could hardly breathe, she knew beyond a doubt that he wouldn't hurt her.

"Please," she added quietly.

Marc took a step forward, and she turned, leading them into her bedroom. Although at that moment, if she didn't think it would hurt her hand, she would have liked to belt him right in the gut.

Moving to her laptop, her fingers shook, in spite of her silent order to remain calm. She managed to bring up her article, then turned, looking up at him, as she pointed to the screen.

"See? I've deleted what I showed you. I'm rewriting it."

His uniform strained over the bulging muscles in his chest. Marc was a giant of a man, and she imagined he could be ruthless if need be. A creature existed inside him that was more than any man's demon could ever be. And it was that creature that would prevent him from losing his temper, allow him to understand her. She envied him that release. It made werewolves more human than humans.

"Why did you do that?"

She was sure it was the amount of control he exerted that made his muscles bulge as if any moment he would transform before her eyes.

Suddenly her nerves consumed her, making her shake. She told herself that it wasn't because he was so damned intimidating. He wouldn't hurt her. She knew he wouldn't. Nonetheless, she wrapped her arms around her chest, hugging herself, and stared at his giant feet.

"I told you…" she began, and then suddenly fought for her thoughts when her mind went blank.

He was too much man—too much werewolf. She took a deep gulp of air, searching for the answer she'd rehearsed to tell him before.

"Because I think I can make a difference. Because I want to make a difference. And I know I can do it."

Someone knocked on Heather's door and Marc turned, sniffing the air. He smelled stale perfume—it was a woman. The hairs on the back of his neck straightened. Something wasn't right.

Heather ran her hands down her suit pants, and then over her hair. She hurried past him, not saying anything but heading toward the door.

Marc turned and glanced at her laptop screen. Half sentences and partial paragraphs were the notes she'd taken in rewriting her article. She hadn't gotten very far. It appeared she didn't know how to begin. One paragraph caught his eye.

I've met a werewolf. And I've fallen in love. Here is my story.

Well, hell.

The second she opened the door he smelled fear and his instincts kicked in. Protect Heather.

"Margot…hello." Heather sounded surprised to see her.

"There's something you need to know. I just found out. You're my friend and I had to hurry over here and tell you. It's not good." Margot paused, catching her breath. "Is he still here? There's a police officer's car in the parking lot. Is that his?"

"Good grief. What is it?" Heather asked, her tone suddenly alarmed.

Marc moved to the doorway, just out of view, but able to see a blonde woman about Heather's age in her living room. The woman wore jeans, and she twisted her hands together in front of her, looking around the room before licking her lips and focusing on Heather. He recognized her as one of the women Heather had been with at the coffee shop.

"It's about that man you're seeing. Oh, Heather. This is really terrible. And I just don't know how to tell you." Margot looked around the living room, her nervousness filling the room with its obvious smell. "Is he here?" she asked again.

"Calm down. You aren't making any sense." Heather put her hand on her friend's shoulder. "There's nothing terrible about Marc."

Margot nodded her head vigorously, her face paling. "Heather...he's a werewolf."

Marc took a step forward, so that he could be seen in the doorway. The living area was full of the stench of fear and panic.

Instantly Margot's hand went to her mouth while she stifled a cry.

"Margot. It's okay." Heather squeezed her friend's shoulder but Margot backed away from her.

Her eyes were so wide they bugged out of her head. She looked from Marc to Heather while backing up until she reached the door.

"Heather," she hissed, opening the door and giving Marc a worried look. "Are you okay?"

"I'm fine. There isn't anything to worry about."

Then Margot curled her lip, looking down at Heather and then back up to her face. "That's sick," she said, and then turned, giving him a final look before shutting the door quickly.

Heather let out a loud sigh and leaned her forehead against the door for a moment.

"Are you sure you're ready to fight this battle?" Marc sensed her aggravation. It filled the room like the spicy smell of anger.

So many emotions clogged the small living area that it was almost hard to breathe. He had the urge to open a window, but instead focused his attention on Heather. So small, yet so strong. And now he would find out exactly how tough she was.

Her hand balled into a fist at her side, and she took her time turning around. "I want to run out and talk some sense into her," she finally said.

Her head was held high, her jaw set with determination. Fire danced in her eyes. He hoped she had the courage to take this on. If she did publish that article, scenes like this would grow in leaps and bounds. For a tiny little thing, he had to give her credit, she radiated with the energy to not back down. And damn, he liked that about her.

"You can talk to her tomorrow." He moved in, watching her take a moment before her focus was on him.

She looked up as he came closer. Confusion warred with frustration on her face. "Your pack doesn't hate me."

"My pack doesn't fear you. And we've always known humans existed."

The way she nibbled her lower lip, digesting his words, looked damned fucking good. He took her chin in his hand, cupping it while he tilted her face. Her lashes fluttered over those sultry green eyes.

The frustration still lingered around her. But its smell was softened by her desire. Just touching her hardened every muscle inside him. His sweet little bitch not only brought out every protector's instinct he possessed, she also made him want to claim her over and over again.

"I guess humans have always needed time to adjust to something different," she said on a sigh.

Decades of time, he thought to himself. But he wouldn't discourage her. Her heart was in this, and that was what he'd ached to see. He'd been outraged when he'd thought she was using him and his pack to better her career, make a name for herself. There was no denying that had been her original intent. She had goals, dreams, and he'd allow her that. But he'd needed to see that she was sincere toward him. That she wanted him.

Had she truly fallen in love with him?

Marc didn't believe in love at first sight—or second sight for that matter. But there was an infatuation, an interest, and it went beyond writing that damned article. Whatever he felt for her, or whatever she felt for him, he would allow it to develop, for now. There was no way he'd turn his heart loose though. Not when their potential relationship rested on such shaky ground.

"So why did you follow me home?" she asked.

"Lock your door."

He felt her swallow, saw the glaze of desire darken her eyes. She turned, latching the door, and then moved quickly past him into her small kitchen area.

"Are you thirsty?" Heather pulled open her refrigerator, which he noticed immediately was almost bare.

No wonder the woman was so damned tiny. His mother never would have allowed their refrigerator to be even half that empty. A trait he'd carried with him as an adult. If anything, there is always food in the cupboard, his mother would say.

Reaching over her, he shut her refrigerator then turned her around.

"All I want right now is you."

"That's why you followed me home?" A small smile appeared on her face.

The frustration was gone. No more aggravation lingered in the air. Her wonderfully sweet smell of lust, of passion and desire, intoxicated him.

"Damned good reason if you ask me."

Already he'd pulled her suit jacket off of her. Her lace bra showed through her silky white blouse. The view made his blood pump harder through his veins. His muscles hardened with restraint while his cock bounced to life painfully in his uniform. His fingers shook with the urge to rip the blouse from her body.

She appeared to read his mind. Her tiny fingers raced over the buttons, undoing them, offering him the view he craved to see.

"You are one hot little bitch," he growled, reaching to unzip his trousers. His cock needed freedom more than he needed to breathe.

Heather moistened her lips, and he couldn't take it any more. He pounced on her mouth. Lifting her into his arms, he impaled her hot, moist mouth with his tongue.

The way she gasped made his muscles quiver with the urge to grow. Need rushed down his spine sending the fine hairs on his human flesh into red alert. Her hands brushed over his shoulders, touching him, caressing him, making his nerve endings incredibly sensitive.

Her hands moved between them, somehow managing to finish unzipping his pants. When her small hands wrapped around his cock, everything around him tilted to the side.

"Damn it." He needed her so desperately he couldn't think straight.

His fingers fumbled over her pants, that hot pussy of hers being too damned confined. When he was about ready to simply rip the zipper free of the material, her soft, small hands covered his, moving in to take care of the task. He pulled his belt from his pants, placing his gun and cell phone on her table behind him.

"I need you, Marc," she whispered into his neck.

Her breath sent chills rushing over him. His cock grew, pulsed, inflamed with desire to bury himself deep in her hot little cunt.

"You've got to let me down so that I can get out of my pants and hose." Her breathing came in pants and her hair was messed up when she pulled away to look him in the eye.

"No, I don't."

Her smile almost undid him. "Yes, my dear. Just for a second. You can't destroy my work clothes."

He allowed her to slide down his body. Her breasts rubbed against his chest, so damn fucking soft and perky.

A cloud of need fogged his senses. But he'd have to give her credit. Heather managed to slide out of her pants and pantyhose in record time. He was a bit more awkward with his shirt, managing somehow to get it off without stripping every button from it.

"Come here." He grabbed her, lifting her again into his arms.

She wrapped her legs around his waist, positioning her already damp pussy over his cock.

Her ass rested against the counter and she wrapped her arms around his neck, looking down as his throbbing cock nestled into her heat.

He thrust—hard. Heather let her head fall back and cried out as he buried himself in her as far as he could go. She was wet, so fucking hot, and tight enough that he could hardly breathe.

Sliding her blouse off of her shoulders, he cupped her breasts, kneading them while her nipples hardened like jewels against his palms. He nipped at her neck, driving into her heat with his cock while she held on tightly to his shoulders.

Her bra had to go though. He needed flesh, had to feel her. A quick tug ripped the thing from her body.

"Oh, hell yeah." Apparently she'd quit caring about her clothes. "Ride me hard, my werewolf."

Marc's blood boiled through his veins at her words. He gripped her ass, straightening so he could watch his cock glide in and out of her moist heat. Heather's cunt muscles gripped his shaft. Her white cream soaked his flesh, filling the air around them with thick, ripe lust. With every breath he grew more drunk on her.

"I want to go deeper." He pulled her legs from around his waist, wanting—no, needing to bury as much of him as he could inside her.

"Oh shit. Marc." Her body fell back on the counter, her head landing against the window over her sink when he pulled her legs up and rested her ankles on his shoulders.

Holding her tight, he began moving his hips, letting her cunt caress his cock. Damn it, if she didn't feel so incredibly fucking good.

She gripped his arms, her fingers digging in as she held on and took all he could give her. Sweat glistened over his body, making her legs slide over him as he plummeted deeper and deeper into her tight heat.

Heather turned her head, reaching for her faucet, and let go of him long enough to turn on the water. Cupping her hand underneath the flow, she splashed cold water on his chest, soaking both of them.

Marc howled. The coolness shocked his senses, fed him with a new life, and made his cock harden painfully inside her.

"You little bitch," he said, unable to hide a grin.

"Thought you needed cooling off," she managed to utter between pants.

She tossed more water on them, soaking them, the counter, the floor, which made her laugh. He wanted her crying out his name, not laughing while she played with water. He was giving her everything he had. She shouldn't be able to move.

Leaning over her, driving in hard and furiously, he rode her with more strength than he knew his human body could muster.

"Oh fuck!" Her nails dug into his skin, burning him as she scraped her hands over his arms.

But he had her attention. The water continued to run but their wet bodies slapped against each other while he showed no mercy.

"My sweet, hot, little bitch." He could barely speak.

His cum rushed through him so furiously that he couldn't have stopped it if he'd tried. Never had any female ever brought him to such a quick and hard climax. Growling until his throat hurt, he filled her with everything he had.

It took a moment to straighten. His muscles spasmed in his cock, hard and swollen deep inside her. When he raised himself off of her, she remained collapsed on the counter, her eyes closed, her breathing heavy.

"Are you okay?" he asked, enjoying how her perky breasts heaved up and down as she worked to catch her breath.

"Not sure," she mumbled, still not moving.

Marc cupped his hand under the running water in the sink next to her and then poured it over her breasts. Her nipples hardened like round pebbles.

"Bitch," she cried out, opening her eyes wide as she straightened quickly.

"I thought you didn't like that word." He was still stuck deep inside of her and her movement made her pussy muscles contract, stroking his cock.

"Do that again and it will become my pet name for you," she threatened, giving him a dirty look.

He laughed and then lifted her off of the counter, his cock in no hurry to leave her warm haven. She wrapped her arms and legs around him and then nestled her cheek against his shoulder. Never had he been more relaxed with a woman.

Chapter Thirteen

&

It was mid-week before Heather saw Margot again. Entering the snack room in the basement of the newspaper, she spotted Margot sitting at one of the square tables. Margot looked up when Heather approached.

"Are you still mad at me?" Heather asked, glancing at Margot, and then Phyllis Bradley, one of their junior editors, who sat next to Margot while munching on a sandwich.

Phyllis looked at the two, raising her eyebrow curiously.

"I'm sorry that I got so upset the other night." Margot waved at the chair for Heather to sit. "Your situation just took me a bit off-guard."

"What are you talking about?" Phyllis leaned in, ready to hear the latest gossip.

"As you can see, I kept your secret." Margot straightened, her expression sober.

She might have calmed down about Marc. But she obviously had serious issues about it. It wasn't like Margot not to spread a good story. An uneasiness spread through her. Heather didn't know whether to be relieved or worried.

She waved her hand in the air, then popped open her plastic container that held the salad that she'd bought for lunch.

"We just had a slight disagreement." Heather smiled at Phyllis.

Margot nodded, reaching for Heather's hand and gave it a tight squeeze. "I'm just looking out for your best interests."

"Well, you two are no fun if you aren't going to share secrets." Phyllis laughed, and then stood up, collecting the wrappings from the food she'd bought out of the vending machines. "See you all at The Zone tonight?"

The Zone was the local bowling alley, and Heather had completely forgotten about it being Wednesday and their night out. Margot nodded, toasting Phyllis with her pint-sized milk container.

"I live for it," she said.

Once Margot and Heather were alone at the table, Margot glanced around at the handful of tables in the windowless room. Heather swore there were days when she could be at the paper all day and never have a clue what it was like outside, or what was happening in the world. Pretty scary for a newspaper reporter.

She followed Margot's gaze around the room and then looked at her friend's dark brown eyes. Margot always wore eyeliner, which enhanced the darkness of her eyes and brought out her creamy white skin. She'd had three kids and still looked so slim in her blue jeans that she wore every day. Margot clasped her hands on the table, the large rock of her wedding ring glistening under the artificial light.

"Have you told anyone else about this?" she asked quietly.

Heather shook her head. Between work and seeing Marc, she hadn't had time to talk to anyone about her personal life.

"Good. Keep it that way." Once again Margot reached for Heather's hand, holding it while she stared her in the eye. "Trust me, Heather. You have such a career ahead of you. All doors are open. Don't fuck it up because you're having a fling like this. Have your fun. Don't get hurt. And keep your head about you."

The wall clock clicked behind Heather, indicating the top of the hour. The hourly employees scooted back their chairs, gathering their trash. The room suddenly filled with noise, and Margot said her hasty goodbyes.

"See you tonight. You're coming alone?" She didn't wait for an answer but squeezed Heather's shoulder and left her at the table with her salad.

Margot had forgiven her and all was back to normal in her small social life. But at what price?

Heather shoved her salad around with her fork, not even looking at it as she stared ahead and allowed what she'd just done to slowly sink in. A nasty knot twisted around in her stomach. And she wasn't sure how to make it go away.

Without a bat of an eye, she'd allowed Margot to think she didn't want anyone to know she was seeing Marc. She'd brushed the subject away in front of Phyllis without letting her know there was a new man in her life.

If he were human you would be bragging about him to everyone.

Suddenly she felt very sick to her stomach.

Marc had thought her shallow, out to use him and his pack to gain a name for herself. And she'd successfully convinced him that wasn't true.

But just now, she'd denied him.

"I really am a bitch," she mumbled, and then leaned back in her chair, knowing there was no way she could eat a thing now.

"There you are," Joey said, making her jump when he hurried into the snack room. "I've been looking for you. Come on, we've got to go. The Community Building is on fire! Front page news! And we get to cover it. Let's go."

His voice echoed through the room as he gestured with his long skinny arms for her to get moving.

Heather tossed her uneaten salad in the trash, and grabbed her purse. "I'll meet you out at the van."

Her heart wasn't in it. It was painfully pulsing in her chest, a mixture of self-pity and annoyance with her behavior making it hard to concentrate. But she had a job to do. Best to throw her energy into it, and figure out later how she was going to handle the knowledge that she was sincerely a shallow twit.

The Community Building was one of the oldest buildings in Prince George, a historical marker. It sat on the edge of downtown, and getting within a block's distance of it at the moment was impossible.

Joey started snapping pictures the second they parked the *Tribune*'s van. Black smoke billowed into the otherwise crisp, clear, blue sky. Pushing through nervous onlookers, the air around her became harder and harder to breathe. A gray hue surrounded everything, stealing the beautiful afternoon and making it appear overcast.

A rope had been stretched halfway across the block, keeping people out while emergency vehicles surrounded the building, fire trucks, police cars, ambulances—all of their lights flashing, adding to the intensity of the scene.

Heather followed Joey, stepping over the rope as she clipped her reporter badge to her shirt. More than likely, it wouldn't get them far. But sometimes the officers assigned to keep out the general public didn't want to bother with them, or didn't know to keep them out.

Enough experience on the job told her not to run around sticking microphones in anyone's face. Her job was to observe, write down the facts, and later create an extraordinary article to inform the town how they'd lost one of their oldest buildings. She would get the facts once the emergency workers were through with their job.

"You know you aren't supposed to be this close." Chief of Police Milburn put his hand out to stop Heather from walking.

She gave him a grim look, having worked with him before, and knowing the man wouldn't kick her out if she followed his rules.

"You still got men in there?" she asked, returning her attention to the still burning building while standing next to him. "Are your guys helping the firemen?"

Fire trucks surrounded the structure, long sprays of water dousing what was left of the building.

"Yup. We got here first. And just one. Already sent two to the hospital." Milburn pressed the mouthpiece to his mouth that he had attached to a phone on his belt. The wires fell down his shirt, and he said something that Heather didn't catch. "I'm hoping we have just about everyone out of there," he told her.

Someone shouted, grabbing the Chief's attention, and he hurried forward. Others rushed toward the stairs as well as someone hurried out of the smoke, obviously carrying another person in their arms.

Joey hurried in front of her, snapping pictures as he went. When the officer who carried a man in his arms, got closer, Heather realized it was Marc.

All she could do was stand and watch him as he hurried down the stone stairs of the burning structure. People rushed around her, everyone talking, but her world came to a standstill.

Marc's blond hair was darkened by ash. His face had black smudges all over it. His uniform was torn, stained with black smudges, and blood streaked down his arm.

Her heart constricted. He had been the one man still left in the burning building. And although he moved quickly, carrying the limp body in his arms to the nearby ambulance, he looked hurt as well.

Everything around her seemed to be a dark haze. All she saw was Marc. Hurrying toward him, she darted around the ambulance technicians and police officers.

"No reporters." One of the technicians blocked her path to Marc with his hand.

Marc was laying the man down on the stretcher while the technicians hurried to get his vitals.

"But...I need to see him." She couldn't focus on anything other than how hurt Marc might be.

Someone was grabbing her arm. Heather turned, her mind unable to focus as Joey tried to drag her back. She fought him off.

"No. I've got to see if he's okay." She tore free of Joey and hurried to Marc before anyone could stop her. "God. You're bleeding."

Marc looked down at her, his expression so serious she couldn't tell if he was fighting pain or not. "I'm fine," he told her.

"You really should let me look at that," one of the men with the ambulance said, nodding to Marc's arm.

"I'll have the pack doctor look at it." Marc turned from the technician, looking toward the building.

"You are not going back in there." She wanted to grab him, make sure that he didn't. But she wasn't sure where he was hurt. Blood had saturated through most of his shirt.

The heat from the fire and the smoke made Heather's eyes burn. They watered and she told herself it was because of the fire, and not tears from fear that Marc was hurt a lot worse than he was letting on. She knew from her research that werewolves had a different metabolism than humans, that they healed at a much faster pace. More than likely he had a much higher threshold for pain.

None of that mattered to her a damn bit. All it meant was that he could be seriously hurt and no one would know because he could control the pain.

He turned to face her as Chief of Police Milburn walked up to them.

"I'm fine," he told her quietly. "Focus on your job."

She sucked in a breath. Damn it. Worrying about him would cause her to lose her front-page story. Since when had she ever allowed anything, or anyone to get in the way of her job?

Joey would kill her if they weren't the main story in tomorrow morning's paper. And her editor would have her neck if she didn't come back with all the facts. She sucked in a deep breath and then almost choked on the smoke.

Marc's arm was around her in an instant, leading her away from the fire.

"McAllister." Milburn was on his ass. "What did you see in there?"

Marc stopped when they'd reached the end of the block and several police cars were parked sideways in the street, stopping traffic. He pushed Heather so that she leaned against the side of the hood.

"The place is completely destroyed." Marc squinted and frowned when Joey snapped his picture.

Heather realized this was her perfect opportunity to get her story. "Do you know what started the fire?"

Milburn had his gaze fixed on Marc, but Heather didn't look away from him. "From what I hear they are saying faulty wiring. But that's unofficial."

As much as she wanted to stay right by Marc's side, be assured that he was okay, there was a job to do. She made a face at Marc's torn and bloody uniform and ached to tell him to stay put, that she would be back shortly. But she knew he would do as he damn well pleased.

"I'll talk to you soon," she said, and then gave his hand a squeeze, a motion that the Chief of Police didn't miss.

She turned to Joey. "We need to find the fire investigator. I need at least a cost estimate of damages, how many were hurt, if there were any fatalities. And do we have anyone from the city here?"

Marc grabbed her before she could leave. "You can find all that out later. I'm not allowing you closer to that building. Once it starts collapsing, it will be even more dangerous than it is now."

Joey wrinkled his brow, cocking his head at Heather when Marc touched her. Well, if she'd denied him before, she was sure being public about him in front of the Chief of Police and her photographer.

Marc's phone rang and he grabbed it, giving her a look that told her he meant business.

"I'll get as many pictures as I can," Joey offered, giving Marc an appraising look before squinting through the smoke toward the building. "Some phone calls later should help us fill in the blanks."

Many times in the past she'd gathered her facts with a few quick calls. From just witnessing this event she knew she could write one hell of a story.

"Go get your pictures then. I'll catch up with you in a couple of hours. I should have something written up by then." Heather didn't have to say anything more before Joey galloped off, not waiting to hear either officer tell him that he couldn't go.

"Go clean yourself up." Milburn turned to head back toward the fire. "You're off-duty for now. Call me later."

"Let me go with you." Heather looked Marc over. "Can you drive?"

Milburn crossed his arms, watching both of them. Marc ignored both of them and headed toward his patrol car parked behind the cars blocking the road. She followed him, noting that he seemed to favor his left arm.

He turned when he reached his car. "Get in."

She didn't ask where they were going, and tried not to stare too hard when he drove mainly with one hand, holding his other one close to his chest. When they'd reached a quiet, older part of town that Heather seldom came to, he pulled into a long drive and stopped the car. When he didn't move at first, she jumped out, running around to the other side to open his door. Whatever pain threshold he had, she had a feeling he'd reached it.

Marc didn't stop her when she held her hand out and offered her support when he got out of the car. There was no way she could hold his weight, but she slipped her arm around his back anyway, holding him close to her as they walked up the path.

An older woman opened the door, and then hurried down the steps of the large front porch. A teenage boy and several small children filtered around her.

"Who'd you fight?" a little boy around five said as he bounced around Marc.

"Thank you, miss," the woman said formally and reached for Marc. "I've got him from here."

"I'm staying with him."

Her words made the woman pause, and she glanced at Marc.

The bright sunny day was such a contrast from what she'd experienced just a few minutes ago. Heather knew she probably looked pretty ashy from the fire.

"Bertha, this is Heather. And she can stay." Marc didn't stop moving, and didn't let go of her as he reached the porch and climbed the stairs.

The children made a path, watching the two of them with wide-eyed fascination.

"She's human, Mom," another boy who looked about twelve said.

"Shush, and get on the phone to his den." Bertha swatted the boy on the head gently, and he ran into the house, the others hovering around their mom.

Heather should have known he would have been going to a werewolf's house. She glanced around quickly, the place seeming clean and spacious, and then guided Marc to a dining room chair that Bertha pulled out for him.

"We've been watching the news," Bertha said, as she began removing his shirt. "I take it you've been out rescuing humans."

Marc grunted, and looked down at his burnt and bleeding arm.

Heather watched in amazement as the woman's hand changed, her nails suddenly growing into long, dangerous-looking claws. She sliced the material of Marc's shirt, and then pulled it gently from his body. Her hand slowly returned to its human form. Heather couldn't believe her eyes. Even though she'd seen Marc change before, this woman had seemed so...normal.

Heather sucked in a breath, the unpleasant memory of how she'd made so light of her relationship with Marc, stabbing at her like a knife to her gut. She had just as bad as an attitude toward werewolves as the readers whose minds she hoped to change with her article.

Bertha ignored her as she moved around Marc. "Natasha. Bring me my bag."

A tall, skinny girl with blonde hair in pigtails scurried out of the room and returned with a large black bag. Bertha worked quickly, applying medicine to the burns and then wrapping his arm and chest with white bandages. She then pulled out a syringe and a small bottle and prepared a shot.

"His den on the way?" she yelled into the other room and one of the kids hollered back that they would be here soon. "Good thing," she said and then poked the top of his arm with the needle. "You won't be driving for a while."

Bertha never spoke to her, or even looked at her, but continued to inspect Marc until she appeared convinced she'd done all he could. Heather stood next to him silently, grabbing the woman's disapproving gaze only once when Heather ran her fingers through Marc's hair, straightening it.

He didn't move, or look up, and she wondered what kind of drug the woman had given him. Bertha huffed, then packed up her bag and left the room. An uneasy silence followed while two of the children moved to stand in the large entryway of the dining room, watching her with sullen blue eyes.

She had a feeling not many humans entered their home. Although she smiled at the kids, neither smiled back, just stood and stared.

A firm knock on the door had all the children running to it, and Heather looked up as Stone McAllister sauntered into the room.

"Well, you're one ugly mess," he told his brother.

Bertha entered behind him, wiping her hands on her plain blue dress. "I gave him a strong dose of hydrocodone. Take him to his den. He'll be fine once he sleeps it off."

"Got it covered. We'll send someone over for his patrol car." Stone gave Heather a knowing look. "You playing nursemaid?"

Bertha snorted. Stone looked away from her, as if not expecting an answer, and reached to help Marc out of his chair. He stood a lot slower than he'd sat down.

Marc let out a string of obscenities, and Bertha slapped him in the gut. "Watch your mouth around my cubs," she scolded, although she didn't sound overly annoyed.

Stone had driven over in a truck Heather remembered seeing parked at his house. Marc insisted on walking outside by himself, but his younger brother matched his pace, moving slowly alongside him. The two were blond giants, incredibly good-looking. Although one looked tired and the other looked too full of anger.

Heather realized he had the same hesitations about humans that she'd had about werewolves. Stone just didn't hide his feelings behind hypocritical comments. So that made which one of them the worse person?

Chapter Fourteen

ℰↄ

Marc's tongue was stuck to the top of his mouth when he woke, and his muscles ached. He lay on top of his covers, staring at his ceiling in the dark, while allowing the cobwebs to clear from his brain.

Bertha and her drugs. Damn it. She'd knocked his ass clean out.

Moving slowly to the edge of the bed, he glanced down at the twisted white bandages that circled his chest and arm. The fire came back to him, the intense heat, screams and cries for help. He'd rushed through that building, smoke billowing around him, trying his damnedest to sniff out all the humans. It had been close to impossible to rely on his senses with the smoke filling his lungs.

Padding his way to the bathroom, he removed the bandages, and took in his naked torso. The burns and cuts had healed, more than likely what Bertha had had in mind. He smelled the fading scent of the antibiotic she'd applied. His pack doctor had ensured no infection would occur and knocked him out long enough for his body to heal. Minor cuts and burns would be mended in less than twenty-four hours with most werewolves.

Looking back into his bedroom at the red digital numbers on his clock by his bed, he realized it was almost midnight. He'd damn near slept twelve hours. Well, a good run would get rid of the sore muscles.

After a quick shower, his mind was a lot clearer.

Heather had been with him when he'd come home. He vaguely remembered Stone driving them here, and his annoyance that Heather had insisted on staying with him.

Stone was a damn hypocrite. His brother would jump Heather in a second, fuck her until she screamed, yet he pretended disgust at the fact that she was human.

He slipped into a pair of boxers when her scent reached him. He hadn't noticed it before. Heading into his living room, he spotted her immediately, lying on his couch, stretched out and sound asleep.

Damn, if she wasn't the most beautiful creature. His insides hardened, a dominating protector's instinct consuming him.

Mine.

Just staring at her, watching her breasts rise and fall slowly, a warm rush of happiness soared through him. She'd stayed with him, making sure he was okay.

One of her hands was curled next to her cheek. Her strawberry-blonde locks streamed across her face. Her lips puckered together, as if she sucked on something, and her long lashes fanned out above her cheeks. Still wearing the clothes she'd had on earlier, he smelled the smoke on her. But even asleep, and with clothes she'd worn all day twisted around her petite body, that womanly scent of hers reached him, hardening his cock.

"My little bitch," he whispered, moving so he knelt next to her. "Time to wake up."

Heather stretched, balling her small hand into a fist as she straightened her arm over her head. Her beautiful green eyes were foggy with sleep as she blinked a few times and stared up at him.

"Marc," she whispered, moving slowly to sit. Her shirt twisted around her, stretching against her perky breasts.

Damn it, she looked good enough to eat.

She looked around the room, squinting, as if she, too, had been drugged and was slowly getting her wits about her. Then her attention returned to him and her eyes widened. She stood quickly, her hands instantly on him, inspecting him.

"I don't fucking believe it," she gasped, and then hurried toward the lamp. "Light. I need light. There is no way you're completely mended yet."

"Darling. Werewolves don't have the same metabolism humans have."

She ignored him, flicking on lights, her hair adorably messed up from her nap on his couch. Focusing on his chest, she returned to face him. When she ran her small fingers delicately over his chest, he fought the urge to grab her. Intense desire ripped through him. Her touch was so soft, filled with compassion and concern, a touch his mother might have applied. Yet he felt the urge to turn it rough, grab her and toss her to the couch, get rid of all those damn clothes she wore.

She turned her attention to his arm, stroking his skin with her palm. When she looked up at him her expression was full of wonder.

"I'm fine."

"That is absolutely amazing." She smiled, shaking her head with her disbelief. "I saw you, bloody and burnt. I can't believe what I'm seeing here. You're all better."

"A little stiff," he said, taking her hands in his and bringing them to his mouth.

He had to taste her, make her scent and taste part of him. Nipping at her fingers, scraping his teeth and tongue over them, he watched her eyes darken while color flushed across her cheeks.

"I'm glad you're better," she whispered, her gaze dropping to his mouth while she sucked in her breath and watched him nibble and lick her fingers.

"I plan on being a hell of a lot better than this here real soon," he told her, his cock so damned hard that it pressed against the restraint of his boxers.

"Oh yeah?"

"Oh yeah."

"What do you plan on doing?" Her tone had turned sultry. She ran her tongue over her lips, creating an urge to simply throw her over his shoulder.

In fact, he did just that.

Heather cried out, surprised, and then started laughing when he turned toward the bedroom, her adorable ass crushed against the side of his face. He gave it a sound smack, and then tossed her on the bed, which was still unmade from his nap.

She fell on her back, her legs spreading, and he reached for her pants, needing to see all of her.

Heather laughed, and quickly scooted out of his reach.

Marc pounced on her, making her cry out once again in surprise, as a fit of giggles escaped her when she couldn't get out of his reach.

Her blouse buttoned down her front, the gaps between her breasts showing a glimpse of flesh. He grabbed the material, and ripped the shirt open.

"Oh shit," she cried, her breath coming in pants.

More than he needed to breathe, he needed her before him, naked, his Heather, on his bed, ready for him.

The bra went next, a quick hard tug ripping the material from her body. Her plump breasts bounced free, her nipples hardening instantly.

"Damn it, you're going to destroy every bit of clothing I own." But her expression showed his actions turned her on.

She was far from annoyed. Her arousal filled the room with an erotic scent that fed his craving to have her.

"And the bad part of that would be?"

"I can't go to work naked," she said, still laughing while she managed to slide backwards and sit facing him.

He was on his hands and knees, ready to devour her.

"Then you will just have to tell them you'll work from home."

Her pants had to go next. He grabbed them at her waist but she swatted at his hand.

"No. I'll take them off. Don't destroy these. They're one hundred percent wool, and expensive."

"Better get out of them then." He backed up on to his haunches, kneeling in front of her, looking down while she quickly slid out of her slacks.

"Happy now?" she asked, tossing her pants and undies to the floor.

She sat cross-legged, facing him, completely naked, and he grinned. Taking in her full breasts, her brown nipples that puckered and hardened as if they called out for him to suck on them, he'd never been happier in his life.

"That's much better." He slid off the edge of the bed, standing and looking down at her.

She gave him a small smile, stretching out on his bed, teasing him, inviting him to devour her. Just the way he wanted her.

"Now you'll stay put. I'm going to go on a quick run. And when I return, I want you spread out on my bed, ready for me, just like you are now."

He turned, enjoying her look of surprise and disappointment. She jumped off of his bed, rushing after him, completely naked.

"Like hell you're going to leave right now," she said, grabbing his arm, but unable to stop him as he headed toward his back door. "I need you. Marc. This isn't fair."

He turned, lifting her in his arms, and kissing her soundly. When he put her down she was gasping, staring up at him mirroring the need that surged through him.

"And when I get back, you are going to perform for me. So you better be ready."

"Perform?" she whispered.

But he didn't elaborate. Let her wonder what he had in mind while he was gone. It would be a damn quick run. He couldn't wait to get back and devour her.

* * * * *

Heather didn't mean to fall asleep. It was too comfortable lying in Marc's bed, feeling the warmth of the sheets from where his body had been. The indention of his head on the oversized pillow, the way the bedspread had been tangled in a straight line down the bed, showed her exactly where he'd slept. And she'd cuddled into that exact spot.

For a few minutes she thought about her article that she'd managed to get turned in to her editor while Marc had been sleeping. She dwelt on Marc's brothers who'd both dropped in to check on him. Stone, with his cold shoulder treatment, and Gabe, with his pleasant manners that was so opposite his brother, in spite of their almost identical looks. There was no doubt though that both of them worried about their brother, and that she might hurt him.

Heather had fallen asleep with that thought putting a knot in her gut. She'd had no problem making her feelings toward him clear in a crisis situation. But when her world was calm, quiet, and her girlfriend had confronted her, she'd denied him.

So what the hell did that mean?

A door closed in the other room. At first she thought it was in her dreams, but then she opened her eyes, taking a moment to adjust to the darkness of the room, and there was Marc, filling the doorway as he stared down at her.

"You are so damn sexy when you sleep." His voice was slightly garbled, and she thought maybe it was because he'd just resumed his human form.

His hair was damp, his body glistening with moisture, and he was completely naked. Corded muscles bulged under his skin. Beautiful blond hair covered his body, thicker on his chest and down his legs. That incredible cock of his stood at attention, as if reaching toward her, eager to reach her.

"I must not have been snoring then." She stretched, intending to tease him, still naked, as he'd instructed.

Marc chuckled, moving closer to the bed. His cock teased her. Just staring at how hard it was, how long and thick, and knowing how he could make her feel, had her pussy pulsing, throbbing with need. Moisture spread between her legs. She could feel it dampen against the shaved folds of her cunt, along her inner thighs. Reaching down, she ran her fingers over her clit, into the depth of her soaked pussy.

"Little bitch," Marc growled, and then reached for her.

Quickly and without hesitation, he took her arm, lifting her from the bed.

Heather scrambled to her knees so that he wouldn't drag her over the covers. Once he had her to the corner of the bed, he climbed on, taking the spot where she'd just been lying.

"If you'd wanted me to move, all you had to do was ask," she mumbled, shaking her head at him.

Marc grinned. "There is something about dragging a woman while she's masturbating that I find incredibly hot."

Heather rolled her eyes. "You are such a brute."

"And you love it."

She paused, heat flushing through her. He'd used the "love" word. And it had hit a nerve inside her. It had crossed her mind to mention that she'd fallen in love with him as her opening line for her article. A hell of a way to grab the reader's eye.

But damn it, if that was her only reason for writing it, then again she was using him. How fucking shallow could she be? Or could it be, maybe just possibly, that she was in love with him and just scared to truly admit it.

"Yes. I do," she whispered, almost afraid to answer him, worried that he might catch her true meaning.

The truth had just hit her, stealing her breath away. She hadn't been so much denying Marc when she had spoken with Margot, as she had been denying her own feelings. Admitting to Margot that she was seeing Marc would have meant admitting how he'd gotten under her skin. Even more than that, how he'd reached her heart.

No one had done that. Her heart was off-limits. Letting go of her heart would be inviting pain. Since she was a child, since her mother had died, she'd sworn she would never allow that kind of pain to touch her again. Yet Marc had done that, and now she risked getting hurt.

Marc's expression sobered, his eyes narrowing on her as if he'd just picked up her change in moods. Suddenly her heart began racing in her chest, the room warming so that her skin felt moist. He could sense her emotions, her feelings. It was like being an exposed nerve ending, laid open for him to do with as he pleased. It terrified and excited her all at once. It was hard to breathe. She wasn't sure at all that she could handle this. But in her heart she knew there was no way in hell she could turn back.

Marc didn't take his gaze from her, as if he were analyzing her. Stretching, he got comfortable while he clasped his hands behind his head.

"Perform for me," he told her quietly.

"Perform?" Her mouth went dry. "What do you want me to do?"

"Masturbate. I want you to masturbate while I watch." He didn't move, his tone remaining serious, while his piercing stare made her heart race. "Imagine it's me touching you while you play with yourself, little bitch."

She kneeled alongside him as he stretched out, his long body spreading easily from head to foot of the large bed.

Muscles bulged, moving under his skin, and she ached to touch him. Reaching out, she hesitated when he shook his head.

"Masturbating means touching yourself, my dear. D touch me."

"Fine." If he wanted a show, she'd give him a show. A he'd be begging for her to touch him before she was done.

His cocky grin egged her on. Not to mention made even more damn horny. Kneeling in front of him she sucked her breath, running her hands over her breasts, down her tummy, and between her legs.

Hot cream soaked her fingers, and she stroked her moi folds, spreading herself open as she slowly moved her hand back and forth between her legs.

Her own motions turned her on, and she closed her eye letting her head fall back while imagining Marc touching he there, stroking her, making her crave his cock.

She arched her back, increasing her movements, gliding her fingers inside her hot cunt. The heat built, while a pressure formed deep inside her, an ache she couldn't appease with her fingers.

Her breath caught in her throat. Her fingers had hit that spot, and she pushed further, encouraging the dam to break deep inside her. It was like reaching that eternal itch, that one part of her that craved attention, needed soothing.

Marc's breathing seemed louder, and she blinked a few times, it taking a moment's effort to focus on him. There was no way she could stop doing what she was doing. It felt so damn good. She ran her hand over her belly, caressing her breast, while she continued to finger-fuck herself.

Marc had grabbed his cock, his eyes glazed over with lust while he watched her play with herself.

"That's it, baby. I want you to come for me." His voice was a deep gravelly sound, his jaw set with determination.

She watched his muscles flex while his arm moved, his long fingers slowly gliding up and down the length of his cock.

He reached for her with his free hand.

She shook her head, her hair falling over her face. "No way, my werewolf. You said no touching. Follow your own rules."

Marc chuckled, his free hand balling into a fist. "Fucking come," he whispered, not touching her, but driving her crazy with his hand so close, reaching out toward her.

Heather couldn't stop her grin. Marc had to be in charge, or feel that he was, and he was happy. She could handle that.

Letting her head fall back once again, she ran both hands over her body, spreading the moisture from her pussy over both of her nipples. Marc groaned, and she knew she had his undivided attention. That knowledge empowered her.

Running her hand down her front, she again stroked her pussy, teasing her clit while the dam inside her continued to threaten to break.

Marc moved on the bed, and she opened her eyes quickly, thrilled with the knowledge that he'd watched as long as he could bear and now needed to fuck her. He reached for her, having moved to his knees, and she grinned.

"Something you want, my dear?" she teased, giddy with need.

"Oh, hell yes." His smile was almost dangerous-looking, his blue eyes brimming with silver. "A better view."

"Huh?" She didn't understand.

Marc grabbed her waist and pulled her further up on the bed. She was still on her knees and he positioned her, while moving to lie on his side. Then he pushed her backwards, so that her back hit the bed although she was still on her knees.

"Like that," he told her, and then spread her legs open further. "Now play, make that pussy drip with cum for me."

In this position she couldn't reach her pussy as well but began stroking her clit, the small movement making her insides throb. His long fingers pressed against her inner thighs, but she could barely see over her arched torso to tell

where his head was. She imagined he had a damn good view though.

If his growls were any indication, he was loving the hell out of this.

He pushed her legs even further apart, and her inner thigh muscles stung from being stretched so far.

"Spread yourself open, my little bitch. Oh, hell yeah. That is one fucking hot view." His raspy whisper was almost too deep to hear.

"Marc. I can't take it anymore. I need more than this." She was absolutely going to go nuts if all he did was watch and not touch her.

Masturbating was something she did when she didn't have a man. But she had Marc. And she didn't want to use her own hand anymore. She wanted his cock. Plain and simple. He needed to fuck her.

A cry escaped her lips when his fingers slid up the insides of her legs, his hands moving over hers. She slid her hands up her body, anxious for him to take over, to feel his rough, determined touch.

He pressed against her swollen and wet pussy, stretching her open. "Come back here, little bitch. Play."

She groaned. "You do it."

"No, my dear. You are going to make yourself come."

"I'm too horny to do that." She knew that didn't make sense and that she was whining, but she didn't care.

Marc chuckled, taking her hand in his and bringing it back down to her clit. "Rub right there."

He had her spread wide open with his fingers while she caressed her swollen and throbbing nub. Her body convulsed, and if she were more limber she would have pulled her body up from the position he had her in.

Need rushed through her. The dam finally fucking broke. Heather about came off the bed, the muscles in her legs straining while needles seemed to rush down them as she exploded against their hands.

"That's it, baby. Oh, hell yeah. I knew you could do it." His praise made her come even harder.

The room started spinning, and she rolled to her side, scared she would black out from the intensity or her orgasm.

Marc lifted Heather, unable to wait another moment. Watching her get off like that had been torture like he'd never imagined. Her sweet little pussy had pooled with thick, white cream. And when it seeped out of her, while her muscles convulsed, he thought he would explode right there.

"Marc. Dear Lord. That was incredible." Her smile was sleepy, sated.

"You're not done yet." He would die if she told him she needed to wait.

She smiled, the glow in her face adding to the torture that already ransacked his system.

"I'm done doing the work," she said coyly. "Now it's your turn. Fuck me, werewolf."

He didn't need her to suggest that twice.

She was so relaxed in his arms, still breathing heavy, her body aglow with lustful energy. Her scent was like nectar, an intoxicating aroma that made him mad with need. Every muscle in his body was hard, not just his cock.

Laying her down gently on her back, he climbed over her, moving his arms under her legs so that he lifted her to him. Her ankles rested easily on his shoulders, that sweet smell of her pussy robbing his senses of all rational thought.

Adjusting himself, he plunged easily and quickly into her hot little cunt.

"Oh shit," she cried out, fisting her hands into the bedspread on either side of her.

"Damn." Her heat wrapped around his cock, and then soared through his body like a beautiful poison, intoxicating and capable of taking over every inch of him.

And that was what this little vixen had done. He realized that. Gliding against her inner muscles, her heat and dampness wrapping around him, he wondered at the fact that just after a two weeks, he didn't want to live without her.

Cariboo know their mates the second they see them. It's in our nature, his mother used to tell him. He could only imagine the expression on her face when he brought a human woman home to his parents' den.

Gritting his teeth and taking her ankles in his hands, he spread her open while he slowed himself to a steady movement.

Heather lashed her head from side to side. "You're going to kill me," she moaned. "I just know it.

She tried to wiggle under him, but he maintained his slow pace. For just a few moments, he wanted his head clear, needed to enjoy every bit of her.

Her body glistened with moisture, and her breasts were beautiful creamy mounds, so perfectly round with adorable brown nipples that at the moment were like hard temples designed for him to adore.

He let go of her legs, and she quickly started moving her ass to liven up the speed. Ignoring her efforts, he lowered himself, and nibbled on one of her tits.

"Marc!" she screamed, her hands moving to dig into his shoulders.

He grabbed her wrists and pinned them to either side of the bed.

"Damn it. Fuck me harder." Her eyes glowed an intense emerald shade when she opened them wide, staring up at him.

"I thought you were worn out," he said, moving from one nipple to the other.

"That doesn't mean I don't need to be fucked."

Marc chuckled, loving her craving for him. "You like my cock, little bitch?"

"I love it," she cried out.

He slammed deep inside her, instantly picking up the momentum, knowing it would do him in, but needing to give her what she wanted. Her pussy constricted around him, soaking him while she screamed, her hair fanning over her face.

Relentless, giving her everything he had, he drove into her repeatedly until her heat had completely consumed him.

She cried out, tossing her head from side to side, fighting the restraint he had on her hands, while her body convulsed underneath him.

"Damn it. Woman." Never had the tightness of a hot little pussy controlled him as much as hers did.

Her rich scent, lust and that smell that was so uniquely hers, took over his ability to think straight. His body hardened, his cock growing until he thought he would explode clear down from the base of his shaft. When he let go, unloaded deep inside her, he came so hard his muscles quivered throughout him.

A growl escaped from deep in his lungs, causing him to arch, throw his head back, and howl while the beast and man filled her with everything he had.

His muscles convulsed so hard that he almost lost control, the change aching to rip through him and take over. Such strong emotions and carnal instincts warred with the man inside him.

His teeth stretched against the inside of his mouth, while little hairs prickled over his skin. Pumping everything he had inside her hot little cunt had his muscles twitching, craving the change.

He locked deep inside her, unable to move, so completely drained that for a moment he didn't have the strength to stop the natural beauty of the beast from taking over. Even as his mind battled his body, telling it that she was human, that she wouldn't be able to handle him changing while inside her, the physical need to do so fought back.

A werewolf bitch would know that fucking her so thoroughly, unloading so completely that the beast within tore free, would be an honor and a statement of how thoroughly he'd given himself to her.

Another growl escaped him, his still-hard cock dancing inside her, locked deep within her cunt.

"No." His mouth didn't want to move right to say the simple word.

Her small hands were on him, brushing gently over his tortured flesh. His senses had heightened, and he saw her emotions as well as her flushed expression.

"Shh…" She pursed her lips together, her eyes wide with wonder but her expression calm. "It's okay."

Was she telling him she didn't mind if he changed while on top of her? Or was she trying to calm him so that he would remain human?

Marc couldn't tell. Primal emotions preoccupied his mind, had consumed his rational thoughts. The natural, more carnal side of him had the upper hand.

Knowing he probably couldn't utter any words at the moment, he managed to lower his face to hers, brush his cheek against her satiny flesh. Her scent robbed all thought from him, rational or otherwise.

His woman. His bitch.

She would learn to accept him as he was. Werewolf or man. No matter what his form she would love him, belong to him, be proud to have him locked so deep inside her, mated as werewolves had done for centuries.

Marc lifted his head, feeling his cock slowly soften, and raised himself so that he knelt on the bed. Her legs slid down him, her body sated and glowing with the aftermath of incredible sex.

He closed his eyes, thinking that she'd just been smiling at him, but unable to trust his senses in their mixed-up state.

When he slid out of her, he backed off of the bed, and headed for the bathroom. His muscles twitched in his legs, resuming their human form while he pushed himself. Splashing some cold water on his face might help. Hell, maybe a cold shower would completely bring him back to his senses.

What the fuck had he just been thinking?

Like hell, Heather would ever be able to handle him as a complete werewolf, or even half-changed. She was a damn human, and unaccustomed to what he took so naturally, to the true beauty of the creature inside him that made him whole.

He didn't mean to slam the bathroom door, but his muscles were still too large for his body. Flipping on the light, he stared at himself for a moment in the mirror. His blond hair stood on end, streaks of white, coarser hair running through it. His mouth was too large for a human face, and long incisors pressed against his human flesh. Muscles bulged under his skin, rippling and cording around his bones that he'd managed to keep in human form.

The door opened behind him, and Heather's image appeared in the mirror next to him. She was so small, so petite with her strawberry-blonde hair messed up and her naked body smelling of damn good sex. Quite possibly, she was the most beautiful creature he'd ever laid eyes on.

"Are you okay?" she asked quietly, and then she touched him.

His skin was still too sensitive, the beast in him not wanting to go into remission. Her scent wrapped around him like a warm blanket, and he realized he didn't smell fear, or repulsion. She was concerned.

He looked down at her. "This is who I am." His voice had almost returned to normal.

Running his tongue over his teeth he realized they had almost receded to their human form.

Heather nodded, and looked down at his body, her tongue running over her lips. "You got up like you were mad or something."

"It's hard to restrain from changing when emotions run so thick through me." And possibly she could live with that. After all, she hadn't run from the room screaming in terror.

A rush of emotions escaped from her, filling the small bathroom with a mixture of smells. He brushed her hair back, needing to see her expression.

"I'm flattered that you experience so many emotions when making love to me," she said quietly, still not looking up at him.

"You should be."

She did look up then, and he saw the moisture in her eyes. Humans might not have the completeness, the freedom, to thoroughly express their emotions and release them, but at the moment, she was doing a damn good job. He just didn't understand the mixture of smells coming off of her.

She waved her hand in front of her face, the sour smell of her embarrassment, as tart as the smell of lemons, filling the bathroom.

"Well, it was damn good sex." She turned, leaving him and reentering his bedroom.

He followed quietly, watching her adorable naked ass when she stopped in the middle of his room.

"It's late. Get to bed."

She turned, and he caught a glimpse of a lone tear streaming down her cheek. He should go to her, hug her, console her while whatever emotions surged through her ran their course.

"You want me to stay?" Her embarrassment lingered but he could tell by her small smile that she liked the idea.

"Get in bed." Instead of holding her, he simply crossed his arms, watching while she climbed into his bed and pulled the cover over her.

Mine! His body hardened once again with the knowledge that he had no desire to ever let her go.

Chapter Fifteen

ဆာ

Heather sat at the bar the next evening, staring down at the front page of today's paper, unable to hide her smile.

"You two should be proud," Stephen, her boss, said, and then guzzled some more of the beer he had in his hand.

Joey put his arm around her. "What can I say? We're just damn good."

Heather laughed, knowing it was a good article, one of the best she'd ever written. She looked at the color picture on the front page. Joey had captured the intensity of Marc as he'd carried that person out of the burning building.

Over lunch, Marc had stopped in at the paper, carrying a copy and strolling through the newsroom like he'd owned the place. Several of the ladies had stopped him, asking him to sign their paper. He'd been as gallant as a movie star, saying nothing but willingly doing as they bid.

Then he'd strutted right up to her desk. "It's lunchtime," he'd told her.

She'd shook her head at him. "You've got a hell of a way to ask a lady out," she'd teased.

"Let's go," he'd growled.

It hadn't bothered her a bit to walk by his side through the building to his car. In fact, it had felt damn good — pretty close to perfect. The rest of the afternoon, after she'd returned to work, had sailed by. She'd willingly agreed to do drinks with her boss, although she couldn't wait to go find Marc.

"Your werewolf angle sure captured attention." Stephen kept on talking, but she didn't hear the rest of what he said.

Gabe McAllister strolled into the bar, his large physique grabbing the attention of more than one woman as he strolled toward her. He took her in with a long, slow look, his attention riveting on Joey. For a second, Heather thought she heard him growl.

With the music playing from the CD player, and all of the chatter in the somewhat crowded bar, she knew she probably imagined it. It was the way his expression hardened, just the way Marc's did when something didn't please him.

She smiled at him, nodding, wishing she could quickly explain that the men with her were simply co-workers. But she didn't owe Gabe any explanations.

He nodded at her, not smiling, and continued past her. She turned, watching as he joined a group just a few barstools down along the long bar.

"You've got something going on with that werewolf, don't you?" Joey's question through her off-guard.

For a moment she thought he meant Gabe. Then she realized he was talking about Marc, and her article. She licked her lips, remembering how she'd brushed Marc off when talking to Margot.

After last night though, and experiencing both sides of Marc at once, knowing that his emotions had bettered him, brought out the beast in him even when he'd fought to keep it at bay, she hesitated. Looking up at Joey, knowing his question wasn't meant to pry but simply in earnest, she nodded slowly.

"Yeah. I've got something going on with him." Her voice was barely above a whisper but Joey heard her.

He didn't smile, didn't look repulsed, but simply gave her shoulder a squeeze. "Well, good luck," he said.

Something lifted off of her shoulders. Heather instantly experienced a rush of giddiness, and the urge to start laughing hit her hard enough that she put down her drink, thinking she'd probably had enough. But she knew it wasn't the alcohol, and it wasn't the success of her article. For the first time, she'd openly admitted to her relationship with Marc. And it felt damn good.

"Thank you," she said, and couldn't stop the grin she knew spread clear across her face.

Joey shook his head, and then tousled her hair. "I've never seen you have the hots for a guy before. You look downright silly."

"Thanks a lot," she grumbled, doing her best to put her hair back in place but unable to stop smiling.

"This guy here?" Stephen was obviously a bit slow. He tapped the newspaper on the counter with his stubby finger. "You are seeing a werewolf?"

He spoke loud enough that several people around them turned and looked. She straightened, taking a deep breath. She could handle this. She had to handle this.

"We just started seeing each other." It was the first thing that came out of her mouth.

She told herself she wasn't downplaying the situation. It was the truth. In over a week, she'd fallen hard for Marc. Where it would head, she had no clue. But there would be no denying the fact that feelings existed, and they were mutual. The way she'd moved him last night, brought out such raw emotions that he wasn't able to hide, made him a better man than any human could be.

She'd realized that when he'd almost changed while fucking her. Most human men could stifle their feelings so well that even after years of marriage you could hear women comment on how little they knew their husbands. But with Marc, emotions took over and it brought out the werewolf in him. She had the advantage of knowing when she'd affected him. Such a blessing was something she wasn't sure she ever wanted to let go of.

Stephen scratched his stomach, successfully managing to untuck his work shirt even further from his slacks. He frowned at her.

"You're actually dating a werewolf?" This time when he spoke, the group of people around them at the bar stopped talking, glancing from her boss to her.

Heather felt the heat rush over her cheeks. Joey took his arm off of her and shifted from one foot to the other.

"Don't make such a big deal out of it." He tried to lighten the moment. "She can do what she wants with her personal life."

Heather was all too aware of several people around her staring at her, and then the whispering started. Her stomach twisted in knots, and she put her glass of beer down on the bar counter. She wasn't sure she was ready for Stephen to make a scene over this.

"Not when you hit the front page." Stephen put his glass of beer down too. He scowled at her. "If I had known this article hit such a personal level because you were talking about your boyfriend, things would have been different."

"How would they have been different?" Heather asked. "The facts are accurate. It's a damn good article. You can't deny that."

"That's not the point. The last thing the newspaper needs is bad press because its best journalist is doing a werewolf."

"That's not fair." She said the first thing that came to mind, which she had always done when she got mad about something. "I'm a good writer. That article has nothing to do with my personal relationship with Marc."

She managed to keep her voice low, wishing more than anything that they weren't having this conversation in a crowded bar. And that so many around them seemed to be obviously eavesdropping. More than anything she wanted to turn around again, assure herself that Gabe was far away from them, that he couldn't hear their conversation.

Werewolves have heightened senses. He's probably easily hearing every word.

168

"You may see it that way. But think about the public, Heather." Her boss was suddenly all business. He shoved his stubby fingers into his pants, working to straighten his shirt. He didn't succeed in tucking it all the way in, but shuffled around in the effort. "If word gets out that you wrote that article, and your impression of being able to get into the mind of a damn good cop are actually because you're sleeping with a werewolf…well, that just won't sit right."

"What I do, or who I see on my own time is my own damn business." Now Heather did raise her voice. She didn't like where this conversation was heading — not one damn bit.

"No, my dear. That isn't how it works. You want the fame of being a successful journalist, then you take my advice. Keep your ass clean. Break it off with that werewolf." Stephen gave her that look that she knew all too well. "Humans and werewolves just don't mix." He sliced the air with his hand. "Everyone knows that."

It was the way he turned his lips into a thin line. The hardened expression he gave her. He was royally pissed off. "You two have a good night. Suddenly I'm not in the mood for drinking anymore."

Stephen turned, and headed out of the bar. Heather turned, her entire insides collapsing as she sighed heavily and rested her elbows on the damp bar counter.

"This isn't fucking fair." She ran her fingers over her face, hating the fact that she was in public at the moment. "Joey, I'm going to get out of here too."

"You want me to give you a ride home?" He gave her back a quick massage, as always, the good buddy she loved working with.

She shook her head, remembering at that moment that she'd ridden with him from work to the corner bar.

"I think the walk back to my car might do me good right now." She stood, and then reached into her purse to grab some cash for her drink. "All I want to do at the moment is wring

Stephen Boswell's neck. He has no right to tell me how to live my life."

"Maybe if you just keep a low profile about it," Joey suggested, and then shrugged.

She was glad at least that he didn't judge her. Giving his arm a quick squeeze, she turned to leave. Her attention riveted down toward the end of the bar where Gabe had gone. He was surrounded by a group of women, all of them appearing to adore him while they laughed easily at something he'd just said. But he turned, giving her his full attention. She looked away quickly and hurried out of the bar.

The cold night air shocked her senses, but it felt good at the same time. The downtown area was well-lit and there were a fair amount of people walking the sidewalk considering it was dark, and would only get colder as the night wore on.

She hadn't made it half a block when loud footsteps behind her had her looking over her shoulder out of curiosity.

"Who was the human who had his paws all over you?" Gabe caught up with her easily, falling into stride alongside her.

"I'm flattered you left all of those women for me," she said instead of answering him.

"Werewolves take care of their own." He looked down at her with eyes so similar to Marc's.

Gabe was a damn good-looking man. His features were similar to Marc's although his face looked gentler, like he hadn't spent a moment of his life worrying about anything. His words sank into her slowly. Her tummy did a little flip-flop.

"You consider me one of your own?" she asked, and crossed her arms against the night. The cold air wasn't bothering her though. If anything, her insides steamed with anger—anger at herself and at her boss.

"Marc does." He didn't elaborate.

She looked up at him, his expression blank. She couldn't tell for the life of her what he was thinking. It was obviously a family trait.

"Well, my car is just down at the newspaper. You don't have to walk with me."

He didn't answer, just stayed in stride next to her. Locking his hands behind his back, he gave her a scrutinizing stare.

"You didn't answer my question."

"What question was that?"

"Who was that pup who had his paws all over you?"

Heather smiled. She could get real used to this protectiveness. There would have been a point in her life, not so long ago, when she would have told anyone who asked her about her business where they could stick it. And with her boss, and Margot, she might very well still do just that. But Gabe suddenly sounded a lot like Marc. It was like he too was putting a claim on her, allowing her into their small den. She really liked how that felt—like she belonged.

"I work with him. Joey is my photographer."

Gabe didn't say anything, just continued to walk alongside her. She felt like she had an oversized bodyguard. For such a tall man, he moved quietly, making her feel very small next to him.

They reached the next block and continued on in silence. Gabe wore a popular cologne, unlike Marc who never seemed to mess with such stuff. She hadn't even noticed any bottles of aftershave or anything at his house. He was a soap and water kind of guy, needing nothing else than his natural charisma to turn a lady on. Damn, even dirty and in uniform after a day's work, Marc was sexy as hell.

"I'd like to think that your thoughts have lingered toward my littermate, and that the smells of lust on you aren't because of me." It almost sounded like he was teasing her. But when Heather looked up at Gabe, his expression remained masked.

She remembered Marc telling her that he'd shared women with his brothers in the past. Her cheeks flamed with embarrassment and she turned her attention toward the street, hating for Gabe to see her blush.

"I'm not sure I like the fact that you can smell every emotion I'm feeling. It's almost like you can read my mind."

"Who says I can't?" Now he was teasing, she could tell by how his blue eyes suddenly danced with laughter when she quickly looked up at him.

"Well, you aren't so hard to read either, mister. Don't think I don't know why you are walking me to my car." She really had no clue. But she could pull a bluff along with the best of them—at least she hoped that she could. "You don't have me fooled for a minute. You're no gallant gentleman."

"Well, hell, you figured out already that I plan on seducing you?"

She almost tripped over her shoe. Gabe grabbed her arm, stabilizing her while she stared up at him, her mouth suddenly too dry to speak. His touch was gentle, yet firm. With his muscular physique, sporting a skintight T-shirt, and snug-fitting jeans and cowboy boots, there was no doubt in her mind he could have taken home any of those girls at the bar, if not several of them. As short as she was, and still in her work clothes, she knew she didn't hold a flame to any of them. Her mind stumbled for a quick response, and came up lacking. She absolutely sucked at the flirty one-liners.

"Certainly you're accustomed to men hitting on you. Hell, you had two men with you at the bar just now," he said quietly.

"I'm not accustomed to any such thing." She pulled her arm free of his grasp, and started walking faster toward her car. Suddenly she wanted to get away from this chick-magnet. "And I work with those men. We were out having a drink after work, nothing else."

"That's a damn good thing." He nodded, his expression relaxing.

She looked ahead of them again, her mind anything but relaxed. If Gabe had wanted to establish that she didn't make a habit of picking up men, maybe that explained his satisfied expression. Obviously he cared about his brother.

Heather didn't have a lot of experience with a tight family. Hers was anything but that. After her mother died, her father had kept to himself, keeping food on the table, and a roof over her head, but that was about it. Emotions weren't something she grew up with. Caring about family members wasn't something she knew a lot about. She let out a sigh, her insides in such turmoil that Marc's brother walking alongside her put her on edge.

Again her thoughts strayed to Marc. She could ask Gabe where he was right now, change the subject to something she'd enjoy talking about. This was his brother after all, she might be able to learn more about him, learn more about werewolves. Anything to end her embarrassing moment.

"Do werewolves change when they're having sex?" She had the question out before she realized she'd once again touched on a subject that had her blushing furiously.

Gabe would think her an absolute fool before they'd even reached her car.

"I mean…when they're with other werewolves?" she added, deciding she would just have to get accustomed to the heat in her cheeks.

Gabe stopped walking. They were on the edge of the parking lot to the newspaper and she wondered if this was as far as he'd walk her. But when she looked up at him, the stern expression on his face brought her pause.

"Marc changed while fucking you?" he asked, obviously having no problem talking about sex.

Well, she was the journalist. Asking questions was part of her job. She took a deep breath, matching his gaze, telling herself she'd come this far. She would damn well take advantage of being alone with the younger brother and get some answers.

"Well, not completely," she told him.

He looked over her head, seeming to stare into the distance for a moment. "Only when they are mating," he said finally.

"When they're mating?"

He nodded, his manner seeming almost cold suddenly. For a moment, he had the hard look of his twin brother.

"When a werewolf mates, it's for life. We bond and it can't be undone. If Marc has changed while fucking you, then you are his bitch. That can't be reversed."

Her insides flip-flopped so hard that for a moment she thought she might be sick.

"But I'm not a werewolf," she muttered, not sure if she was sick to her stomach from excitement, or fear.

"I'm sure you could take the matter to the pack leader. The law is written down. But I doubt seriously it mentions anything about whether the mate has to be werewolf or human."

Chapter Sixteen

ഇ

Paperwork sucked. Beyond a shadow of doubt, it was absolutely Marc's least favorite part of his job. Sitting behind a desk wasn't his thing. Unfortunately, getting everything done in his car sometimes simply wasn't an option.

And now, after talking to Gabe on the phone, he felt even less like finishing up all of these forms. He needed to get out of here.

More than anything what he needed to do was find and talk to Heather. Gabe never should have discussed such things as mating with her. Granted, from what he understood, she'd brought up the subject, but damn it, that didn't matter. If things were fucked up between him and Heather now, he'd have his brother's ass.

It sounded like several things were brought up in this supposedly brief conversation Gabe had had with Heather. None of them sat well with Marc.

He growled at his computer screen, deleting what he'd just typed. At this rate he'd be here all night.

It seemed like he was all thumbs on his keyboard. But his mind kept straying to what Gabe had told him when he'd called briefly after leaving Heather.

Out of everything Gabe had rambled on about, the one thing that worried him the most was when he'd shared what he'd overheard in the bar.

"She told her boss she was seeing me?" At first Marc had swelled with pride, picturing his little bitch standing there announcing that she belonged to him.

"Yeah, and it pissed him off. He walked out on her." Gabe had explained that Heather's boss had made a small scene, raising his voice loud enough to attract the attention of those around them. "The place was full of humans but a few of our pack were within earshot. She left right after that and I decided it best to make sure she was okay."

That sounded like Gabe, always taking care of everyone. Although Marc wouldn't be fooled into thinking his younger littermate wasn't a bit curious about her too. He didn't come on to the bitches as hard as Stone did, but his smooth, mothering attitude, landed him as much pussy as his twin brother.

"I'm sure you did." He knew he should have been more appreciative. But damn it if he didn't wish it had been him in that bar.

Gabe had chuckled. "I'm not sure she liked hearing that she was mated to you for life."

That had pissed Marc off. "Where the hell would she get an idea like that?"

"She asked me if werewolves changed into werewolves when they fucked each other." Now Gabe was laughing. "I didn't know how to take her question at first."

"You told her that she and I were mated?" He could only guess how Heather would have reacted to that conversation. And nothing he imagined sat well with him.

"I explained how our laws work. She's a human. If you tried to mate with her, I mean, seriously mate with her, well, Marc..." Gabe had paused.

Tiny little hairs tickled the back of Marc's neck and then spread down his spine. Every muscle in his body hardened and he fought to keep his temper at bay. It bugged him that Heather had asked Gabe questions about mating, and not him. Sharing his feelings had never been easy, but this was a personal conversation. Why the hell had Heather sought out his brother, someone she barely knew, and asked him things that were none of Gabe's business?

"I just never would have guessed that you'd go and mate with a human," Gabe had finally said.

Marc growled, pushing "enter" to send the form he'd finally finished to the printer. Damn paperwork. His conversation with Gabe had left him antsy, itching to get the fuck out of here—find Heather.

By the time he left the police department, a half moon sat high in the sky. City lights made it impossible to see the stars but the cold night air washed through his senses. He hurried to his car, anxious to get over to Heather's and talk to her.

Taking her for a mate had been on his mind—a lot. But this wasn't how he would have addressed the matter. The standing between werewolves and humans was so shaky right now. If her job was on the line he had a feeling she would run from him before she would run to him. He knew how much being a reporter mattered to her.

Heather wasn't at her apartment. He even made sure when her car wasn't there by knocking on her door anyway. Her scent was nowhere around the building. Remembering that she'd gone to his house before and waited for him, he hurried home. But his place was dark and quiet.

"Well, fucking hell." Instead of stopping at his place, he continued down the dark country road.

His brothers' den was just down Wright Creek Road, and he pulled into their drive while punching in the numbers to Heather's cell phone.

She didn't answer.

This wasn't good.

Marc didn't bother to knock, but entered the den he'd first lived in when moving out here with his littermates from the Canadian Rockies. Stone lay on the couch and lazily looked up at him when Marc entered. The smell of burgers grilling filtered from the kitchen.

"What did you do to that girl?" Stone asked, giving him a look as if Marc had just royally fucked something up.

"What the hell are you talking about? Where's Heather?" He wasn't in the mood for his brother's righteous behavior.

Stone obviously smelled Marc's anger and frustration because he straightened, rubbing his eyes and then giving Marc the once-over.

Gabe strolled in from the kitchen. "You can't find her?"

Marc's littermates watched him, but he didn't answer, and ignored the two of them as he began pacing the living room. She should have at least answered her phone. The urge to sniff her out consumed his thoughts. Something was up with his little bitch, and he knew what happened in the bar, and then her conversation with Gabe, had everything to do with it.

"None of this would have happened if you'd just kept your jaw shut," he hissed at Gabe, needing to burn off some pent-up anger.

His muscles bulged, stretching the material of his shirt. The urge to change, take his aggravation out on his littermates and then run through the night until he'd found Heather, sounded real damn good.

"You shouldn't have changed while fucking her," Gabe countered.

Stone watched the two warily from the couch, looking like he would pounce into action if the two of them took each other on.

"What I do with my personal life is none of your fucking business."

"Well, your bitch made it my business. I didn't ask the questions, she did."

Marc took a quick step toward Gabe, anger creating a spicy smell around him. Stone stood and moved slowly to stand next to his twin. Marc glared at the twins, so incredibly similar in appearance that they'd fooled many throughout their life. But to Marc, they were both so very different.

"Stay out of this, Stone," he growled.

"We'll find her, Marc." Stone wasn't usually the peacemaker. "But I don't want my meat burnt, and Gabe is fixing food. We'll kick your ass on a full tummy, unless you'd rather spend the time figuring out where your bitch is."

Marc moved quickly, grabbing Stone by the neck before either twin could react. Stone gave him a hard stare, not backing down, or fighting back. Gabe didn't move either, the three of them simply staring at each other for a moment.

Marc shoved Stone backwards, knowing taking out his aggravation on the two of them would accomplish nothing. He turned his back on them, fighting to calm his heated senses, and ran his hand through his hair.

"Tell me again exactly what happened between you two," he said finally, turning around and fisting his hands against his hips while staring at Gabe.

"Did you fuck her?" Stone asked, once again his usual ornery self.

"Hell no." Gabe scowled at his brother, and then shook his head at Marc. "You know damn good and well I wouldn't do that without your permission, Marc."

"No one has fucked anyone." Marc raised his hand. The last thing he needed was to picture her fucking anyone else right now. He just wanted to find her.

He had no doubts that Gabe never touched Heather. Her scent wasn't on him. Besides, his brother spoke the truth. Marc knew that not even Stone would touch either of his littermates' bitches without their permission. He knew that line of respect ran deep through all of them.

"She was upset, Marc." Gabe turned, heading back into the kitchen. "I could smell how frustrated that pudgy human made her feel."

All three brothers ended up in the kitchen, watching while Gabe stabbed at some potatoes baking in the oven. They headed out back to the grill, and Marc stared at the half dozen burgers on the grill. He grabbed the plate waiting for them, and began pulling them off the fire.

"I was simply prepared to walk her to her car since she was unescorted." Gabe crossed his arms over his chest, defending his actions.

"As any of us would do," Stone spoke up, showing his more compassionate side that very few ever saw other than his brothers.

They headed back into the kitchen, and Stone changed slightly, allowing his fingers to grow long, deadly claws. He stabbed at each potato, and shook each of them off onto a plate.

"But somehow you started talking about sex," Marc prompted.

He was beginning to think that the issue of her and him being mated might have upset her more than her job.

Maybe she didn't think her work was in jeopardy. Hell, he hadn't been there. And again he cursed silently the fact that she'd endured such an emotional scene without him. Something told him though that wherever she was, she was upset enough not to answer her phone. That pissed him off more than anything. Heather should be running to him if she were upset, not running away from him.

"She brought it up." Gabe already had his mouth full of meat. He swallowed, and then pulled open the refrigerator door, pulling out a few cold bottles of beer. "I guess you must have freaked her out or something. She asked about you changing while you were fucking her."

"I can imagine that would be a bit much for a human bitch to handle." Stone spoke with his mouth full and then washed it down with a couple of loud gulps of beer. He burped loudly, wiped his mouth with his hand, and then grabbed another burger. "I know you think you're more werewolf than most, big brother. But damn, sounds like you bit off more than you can chew with that little human."

Marc scowled at Stone. His younger brother looked at him with a slightly amused glint in his eye, and dug into another burger. As many times as he'd kicked his younger littermate's ass growing up, he'd think Stone would have a little respect. But after all of these years, it was clear that Marc would never be able to intimidate either of them. Right now though, he needed them. And both Gabe and Stone knew that. Just as he would do for them, the two of them were here for him, and would do whatever it took to help find Heather, no matter if they approved or not. He saw that they accepted her to be his bitch.

"She might have freaked thinking she was stuck with you now. I told her mating was for life." Gabe wasn't teasing. His tone was serious and he met his brother's stare looking concerned. "I told her she could challenge the law if she wanted, since she was human."

"No law is going to be challenged." And he wasn't going to lose Heather.

No matter where she was, he couldn't get his mind to accept the fact that she was hiding from him. Something else was up. And he was going to find out.

Stone gulped down the rest of his beer. "In that case, I say we go find her."

If there was one thing he knew it was that his littermates would back him in any decision he made. And without him voicing it, they both already knew what that decision was.

"Yup. And take your cell phones. The first one who finds her better call me immediately." Marc was already stripping out of his clothes.

He tied his shirt in a knot around his phone, and then headed for the back door. He had already driven through town and not seen her, which meant she must be at someone's house. He didn't know her friends, had no clue where any of them lived. But there was one place he could check, and he would head over there in his fur.

Chapter Seventeen

ℭ

It took a minute for Heather to realize where she was. The sound of a child crying in the other room confused her. And she had to be still asleep because the sounds were more like an infant crying and a puppy whining, all mixed into one. It would make sense after her dreams of Marc, and werewolves, all night long that she would hear a puppy whining when in truth it was actually a baby.

Then she sat up, immediately feeling how stiff she was, and realized she slept on a couch. She'd fallen asleep at the pack leader's house, and obviously, from the blanket that covered her, they had done their best to make her comfortable.

And the noises she heard were a mixture of a baby crying, and puppy whining. Samantha strolled down the hallway, her hair messed up, wearing an oversized nightshirt. Her baby was at her breast, his long white tail sticking out of his tiny outfit.

"Sorry we woke you," she said quietly. "He's in a foul mood until he's fed."

Heather smiled, running her fingers through her hair. "I can't believe I fell asleep last night. You were kind to let me stay here."

"You were really upset, and understandably so. Our ways are different from yours. We figured with all the information we discussed, your mind might be a bit on overdrive." Samantha disappeared into the kitchen.

Everything from the night before came back to her in a rush.

After arguing with her boss for over an hour until her cell phone had died, she knew she wouldn't be able to sleep without some honest answers. And in the state of mind she'd been in, there was no way she could confront Marc with all of her questions. Obviously, he'd already decided how things were going to be.

Heather didn't have any really good werewolf friends, but she knew Samantha was the queen bitch, and that meant that she handled issues with the women in their pack. Well, Heather wasn't part of their pack, at least she was pretty sure she wasn't. But she needed answers, and so nervously had asked to come over.

Samantha had been so friendly, quickly encouraging Heather to stop by. Her mate had left them alone, but Heather was pretty sure that wherever he'd been in the house, he had easily overheard everything that they'd discussed.

Heather stood and folded the blanket she'd slept with and put it at the end of the couch, and then headed to the kitchen.

"Coffee?" Samantha asked, turning to smile at her.

She had her baby in a portable bouncy seat propped up on the kitchen table. At the moment he seemed content chewing on a rubber baby toy.

"I'd love some. It is too weird waking up and not having to hurry to get to work." Heather felt the knot that had been in her gut the entire previous evening quickly harden again. "I really should head home though."

"That isn't right about your job." Samantha spoke with enough conviction that Heather knew she was still upset about hearing that Heather had been fired. "I saw yesterday's paper, that was an excellent article you wrote. Werewolves and humans working together in a tragic situation. It should help all of us make headway. And you have to go and get fired over it."

Heather couldn't agree more that the situation was fucked up. "I'm going to go in and talk to my editor today. Hopefully he's calmed down some."

There was something else she was going to do. She needed to get home and write the article she'd been researching for months now. It burned to get out of her. More now than ever before, she had a story to tell.

Samantha poured coffee and offered Heather a mug steaming with the hot brew. "You need to let me know how you want to approach this situation with Marc. I don't have to go through the laws to know there isn't any fine print to clear up this situation."

Heather nodded. "Well, if in his heart he mated with me, then he should have told me."

"*Cariboo lunewulf* are hardened in their ways. Even a werewolf bitch has a hard time with those men." Samantha smiled, and Heather knew she tried to make light of the situation that was weighing down her heart. Samantha blew on her coffee, eyeing her baby on the table. "I don't know Marc that well. His den and the other *Cariboo* keep mostly to themselves. They are even quiet at the pack meetings. Johann is still working with them to come forward when they mate, or buy land, so it can be put in the books."

Heather understood now that werewolves didn't have marriages the way humans did. Samantha had explained so much to her the night before. When two werewolves were in love, they mated, and it was for life. As long as they had their pack leader's approval, then the mating went down in the books—and the deed was done.

Johann came down the hallway, his boots clicking on the tile when he entered the kitchen. He ran his hand through Samantha's hair, pulling her to him, and then kissing her on the forehead—an act not unlike something Marc would do to her. Heather's tummy flip-flopped while her pussy pulsed just at the thought of him.

"We've got company—again." He looked over Samantha's head and out the kitchen window.

Heather ached to know what he meant by again.

"I thought I heard something." Samantha looked up at Johann, in that silent way couples do when they are communicating through their gazes without speaking.

Again the intimate act made Heather think of Marc. She needed to see him. There was little doubt in her mind that he wondered where she was. And with her charger at home, there was no way she could use her cell phone, or receive calls, while she was here. The longer she stayed away from him, the harder he would be to reason with once she saw him. All she would want to do was jump his bones.

And that was why she needed some time. When she saw him next, they would need to talk. But before she could have that conversation, she needed to have some things straight in her head.

"Who is out there?" she asked, having a feeling she already knew the answer.

"Marc is here. And he was here last night too." Johann straightened, appearing very much in control of any emotions or thoughts going through his head. "You were asleep so I granted you protection."

Heather licked her lips, and then placed her coffee on the counter, her hands suddenly feeling a bit shaky.

"I...I don't want to make a scene in your home." She sucked in a shaky breath, her heart suddenly beating so wildly in her chest she could hardly breathe.

Samantha reached out for her, but then before touching her, turned slightly, and placed her palm on Johann's chest. She smiled at Heather.

"You came to me as a bitch would to her queen. We will continue to grant you protection. Go home. You will be safe." Samantha spoke so solemnly, sounding just like a queen.

Heather's mouth went dry, and she nodded. More than anything she wanted to see Marc. There was so much to talk about. But before she talked to him, there were a few matters she needed to tend to personally, one of them being her job.

Heading toward their front door, she gripped the handle and then turned, realizing both of them were right behind her. Samantha with her infant back in her arms, and Johann with his unreadable expression. They were offering her so much, she knew she needed to be honest with them in return.

"I think I might love him," she said, her voice cracking.

"We know." Samantha said, although neither of them showed any kind of happiness toward her comment.

Instead Johann reached around her, forcing her to take a step backwards, and opened the door, leading the way out.

They were going to escort her to her car.

No sooner had she stepped outside, when Marc stepped forward. Johann didn't rush into him, but moved so he stood between them.

"She's going home. You'll leave her be for now." His tone was so cold, so harsh, that instantly Heather wanted to reach out for Marc.

But this was what she'd asked for, to go home. Werewolves lived by a code that she knew humans could never master. These people had honor, a willingness to fight for what was right in life. They didn't stab each other in the back, but stood behind each other, forming a tight bond—a pack.

"Like hell she's leaving." Marc bolted toward the car, and Johann jumped on him. "Heather!" Marc yelled, just as the two men toppled backwards.

Johann didn't have the strength to take Marc down. Possibly, even in his anger, Marc respected the rank of his pack leader. He backed off quickly, and glared at Johann before turning to look at her.

Heather hadn't meant to look at him. She'd told herself as she walked out of the house that she would go home, shower, give herself some time and write that article. Once her head was clear then she would focus on Marc.

But when he called out her name, she couldn't look away. She met those piercing blue eyes, glowing with a silver edge. His face was hollowed, dark circles under his eyes. His clothes were wrinkled, almost twisted on his body, as if he'd been in them all night, or possibly had just hurried and put them back on. Dark blond hair, appearing a bit dirty, and ruffled, stood on end. He was a wreck.

And never had she seen a sexier man in all of her life.

"You better hurry up and go," Samantha said quietly. "We'll make sure he doesn't follow you."

Heather looked at the compassion in Samantha's face. Standing outside in nothing more than the nightshirt she'd slept in, she still had a stately look about her.

Marc's growl stole her attention from the queen of this pack. She opened her car door, watching his entire body stiffen, as if any moment he might leap through the air and physically stop her. She shook like a leaf but she knew in her heart what she was about to do was right.

"Give me a couple hours, and then I'll come over." She could barely swallow over the lump in her throat.

More than anything she wanted to run to him, be in his arms, feel his strength around her. The pain she saw in his eyes was enough for her to know that he truly loved her. If he'd mated with her without telling her, they would work it out. He would learn that she was a hell of a lot more than just his "little bitch". All of that would take time though, and right now, she had to show her boss what he was about to lose.

* * * * *

It wasn't until several hours later that Heather realized she hadn't even taken time to shower. Hurrying home, her eyes blurry with tears over the image of Marc's torn expression that she last saw as she pulled out of the Rousseau's drive, she'd walked into her apartment and straight to her computer.

More than she needed to breathe, she had to share her story. And now, with her fingers cramping, she sat back and stared at her computer screen.

I've met a werewolf. And I've fallen in love. Here is my story.

The Heather Graham story. A human who entered into the daily life of werewolves, and found her own life lacking.

She saved the file to a disc, and then pulled the CD from her computer. Glancing at her clock, there wasn't much time if she were to make it to work and talk to her editor—her ex-editor.

At the last minute, she remembered her promise to let Marc and Johann read her article before it was published. She hurried and made a couple more copies, and then headed for a much-needed shower.

Chapter Eighteen

ဆ

Marc was just about to kick every last one of these people out of his house. Apparently, Johann didn't feel his littermates were enough to contain him. And the damned pack leader was right. Stone and Gabe leaned against his kitchen counter, chatting with Rock Toubec's mate. After two hours had passed, and Heather hadn't shown up, he'd been hell-bent and determined to go after her.

He wasn't sure which one of his brothers ratted him out, but just when he was about to bolt out his back door, head over to her apartment, Rock and his mate Simone had shown up.

Another *Cariboo*, there probably wasn't anyone else in his pack that could stand a chance against Marc in a fight. Rock would probably be his closest match. Marc would have taken him on, but within thirty minutes after that, Johann arrived as well.

"I think you *Cariboo* are keeping a bit too much to yourselves." Johann had arrived in a foul mood, and was just about to show what a fool he was for making a scene in a den where he could get his ass kicked.

"But you call us in to help," Rock had said, "and we're here, aren't we?"

Marc turned his back on the lot of them. He'd grown up with Toubec in the mountains, but the asshole was playing loyal to the pack leader today. Marc wanted to take the whole lot of them on, tear into them, releasing every bit of his pent-up frustration.

Not only did it make him crazy that Heather didn't show up when she said she would, it bothered him even more that his pack seemed to have taken her side. They were protecting her, respecting her wishes, by being here and making sure he didn't go after her.

He should be thrilled that the pack had accepted her. She was human, yet she'd won their support. At the moment though he just wanted to be alone. And yes, he wanted to go find his little bitch. No matter that she'd run from him, that she hadn't shown when she said she would, even though that made him crazy in the head, he knew deep inside that it wasn't because she didn't want him.

That look she'd given him before leaving Rousseau's den, the way she'd stared, so torn with compassion dripping from her so hard he could smell it across the yard, her feelings for him were as strong as how he felt for her.

Yet something was going on in her life, and she wanted to handle it without him. That would change. Heather would learn to share every bit of herself with him. He couldn't have her any other way. And he had to have her. That much he'd realized in the past twenty-four hours. No matter that they hadn't known each other that long. He couldn't breathe without her. Never would he have believed he could fall in love so hard, so deeply, with every bit of his soul. But that was what had happened. He loved Heather Graham. Loved her so fucking much it was making him nuts not knowing where she was, or what she was doing.

"A car is pulling up." Rock's bitch cocked her head in the kitchen, stilling everyone in the house with her announcement that someone else was here.

They all remained silent, not moving, as each of them listened to quiet footsteps walk up to the door, and then knock.

Marc could smell her sweet scent. He moved before anyone else and pulled open the door.

"Where the hell have you been?" He didn't give a rat's ass that he had an audience.

"I did it!" She grinned from ear to ear, oblivious to his pent-up outrage that she'd ignored him for so long. "I showed them all. And they bought it. Aren't you proud of me?"

Her happiness filled the air around them. And then, much to his surprise, she jumped into his arms, wrapping her small arms around his neck and pressing her moist lips to his.

The hell with his pack members standing around, their amused and bewildered reactions attacking her sweet scent. He didn't want to smell them. He wanted every bit of him to be nothing but Heather. Holding her tight in his arms, he deepened the kiss, feasting on her mouth.

So hot, so wet, every muscle in his body hardened while emotions so raw, so carnal rushed through him. She belonged to him. Thanks to her own doing, to the fact that she'd announced their bonding sex, his pack now viewed her as his mate.

Marc knew that Heather didn't realize she'd instigated the bonding. She had a new understanding of the ways of werewolves. But when she'd shared with his littermate that he'd changed while fucking her, albeit a partial change, well, things like that weren't taken lightly by *Cariboo lunewulf*. Heather had mated with him, had announced their mating, and now his pack was here to witness and ensure the bond was legitimate.

Heather had jumped into his arms, had claimed him once again in public view — with the pack leader present to witness it, no less. In the eye of any werewolf, that was enough to announce them mates for life.

She broke the kiss off just as she had initiated it. Marc wasn't ready to let her go. All anger had washed clear out of him with her overwhelming happiness. There was still the matter of where the hell she'd been, and why she hadn't answered his calls, but for the moment, all he wanted to do was keep her in his arms.

"Oh shit." Heather looked over his shoulder, her sweet smell changing quickly to that of overwhelming embarrassment. "Are you having a...party?"

She slid down his body, making him fight with more strength than he was sure he had at the moment to keep his cock at bay, not let it go hard as a rock in front of everyone.

"When a pack offers its protection, they take it very seriously." Marc looked down at her as she looked from one person to the next, standing behind him in the living room.

She straightened, running her hands down the adorable mini-dress she had on. Through the snug fit of the material, her nipples stood out, like hard little pebbles. Her emerald-colored eyes shone dark with long lashes fluttering over them. She ran her tongue over her lips, moist and swollen from their kiss. Her soft, strawberry-blonde hair fanned freely to her neck, bordering her creamy skin and offering nice accent to the deep blush in her cheeks.

"I got my job back." She grinned up at him, and then smiled, looking quickly beyond him when Samantha shrieked and clapped her hands.

He wouldn't bother to mention that he'd found out that she'd lost it through secondhand news, and not from her as it should have been. Marc wouldn't sound like the heel when Heather glowed with happiness, and suddenly had the room buzzing with comments of congratulations.

She left his arms, and he watched her, his heart suddenly filling with a pride he wasn't sure he'd ever experienced before. Not too long ago she'd been this human filled with all kinds of false notions about werewolves. And now, here she was, strutting into his home as if she owned the place, so petite, surrounded by incredibly powerful werewolves, the strongest of his pack. And all of them grinned at her, hanging on to every word she said.

His heart swelled with pride. Human or not, she had truly become a part of them. And whether she knew it or not,

Heather captured the room, quickly explaining everything and answering all questions as she went along.

"You would have been so proud of me." She turned around, extending her small hand with her perfectly manicured fingernails, and with eyes just for him. "I pranced right into my editor's office. I told him he was a damn bigot, and unless he wanted a lawsuit on his hands, he would promise me right there that I still had my job."

"And that worked?" Samantha asked.

Rock Toubec's bitch, Simone, stood next to Samantha, the two women looking rather amused at Heather.

"Well, no." Heather grinned from ear to ear, turning to face the two bitches.

The group of werewolves stood around the women, all of their attention on his little bitch. She wasn't nervous around them. Adrenaline pumped through her, filling the air with excitement that the others fed off of. Marc wanted to pull her right back into his arms. Whatever her triumph, he would hear her out. Her happiness lightened the weight that had brought him down ever since she'd been kept from him.

"I don't ever want any of you to think I'm ashamed of my kind. But I won't make excuses for us, either. We take a while to come around. And my boss is probably slower than most."

That comment got a bit of laughter, but Samantha shushed them. "Tell us what happened."

"Well, I have to admit to all of you, I sought Marc out because I wanted to write an article. I saw the market was perfect for a human-interest story on werewolves. And I just knew I could make my career skyrocket if I landed an 'up close and personal' story. You know, one of those stories that gets all the inside scoop that everyone is dying to know."

She had everyone's attention. Whether she realized how serious the group had grown, Marc wasn't sure. She continued on, excitement making her talk quickly.

"You all know…well, Marc and I got to know each other." She blushed so beautifully he couldn't keep his hands off of her any longer.

Wrapping his arms around her waist, he enjoyed how she leaned against him, her backside pressed up against him while she continued to speak.

"I showed him my article and he told me it was crap."

"Sounds like something Marc would say," Stone interjected.

"But he was right." She twisted in his arms, sliding her purse off of her shoulder.

The way she moved her ass against him, all he wanted to do was tell everyone to get the fuck out. They could have this conversation after he'd spent a day or two fucking her. Heather didn't seem to notice how she made his cock shift in his pants. She reached into her purse, pulling out a couple CDs, one of which she handed to him, and the other she offered to Johann.

"I rewrote the article. And today, I went into my boss's office, and told him that was fine, if he wouldn't give me my job back, I would take this article I'd just written, an inside story on my experiences with a pack, and contact some of the major newspapers in Canada and the United States." She looked up at him grinning, and then turned her attention to the others. "Our chief editor overheard me, stuck his head in the door, asked about the article. So I showed it to them. They want to run it in this Sunday's paper."

"And they gave you back your job?" Samantha asked, grinning from ear to ear.

"Well, there are some stipulations, but yes. I'm not fired."

She then turned, giving him all of her attention. Her fingertips brushed over his chest, the touch so gentle, yet like fire through his shirt. He grabbed her hands before she could continue with her soft torture.

"I'm sorry that I stayed away for so long. I told my editor the story couldn't go out this Sunday until your pack approved of it."

"What I have to say to you will wait until we are alone." He managed to keep his tone low, wanting only her to hear him.

The others were already talking, heading over to his computer in the corner of his living room and putting the disc in, anxious to see what might be printed about them. None of that mattered to Marc. He took advantage of the small moment when his pack members were distracted elsewhere. Pulling her close, he got lost in those emerald orbs of hers.

"Don't ever leave me out again."

"I won't. I promise." She licked her lips, never once taking her gaze from his.

She stretched up against him, bringing their faces closer together. "There are some things we do need to talk about...when we're alone."

And he was fucking ready for them to be alone right now.

"Heather." Johann grabbed everyone's attention.

He straightened from where he'd been leaning over the computer in the corner of Marc's living room. The others turned, glancing at her briefly before focusing on Johann.

Heather turned in his arms, but Marc had no intention of letting her go. He looked over her head, the gentle smell of her shampoo mixing with the many other aromas about her that combined to make her everything he needed. Her fingers slid into his hand, and he squeezed gently, silently assuring her that nothing the pack leader could say would harm her—not in his den.

Johann's expression was serious. "Tell your editor that I approve of the article. You did an excellent job."

She noticeably relaxed in his arms, looking up quickly with a delighted grin on her face before turning her attention back to Johann.

"Thank you. That means a lot to me."

Johann reached for his leather jacket, which he'd tossed over the back of Marc's couch when he'd arrived. Samantha moved to stand next to him.

"Your den has our blessing, McAllister." Johann gave him a slight nod, while leading his mate to the door.

Toubec wrapped his hand around the back of his bitch's neck, guiding her out as well. Gabe and Stone looked a bit more hesitant. But Marc had news for them. They were getting out of here too. He wanted time alone with Heather—a lot of time alone with her. The twins might have their own unique bond, one that made sharing their women seem to tighten the union between them. But for Marc that was a thing of the past. There would be no other bitches for him, and no other men for Heather. He didn't need anything to tighten what he felt when he had her by his side.

"Wait a minute." Heather stiffened in his arms, putting her hand on his chest, but looking at Johann. "What exactly is it that you are blessing?"

Marc's breath caught somewhere in the middle of his chest. He wouldn't be able to handle her publicly denying him. A bitch had that right to refuse a mating. But everything he'd sensed about her, felt when he was with her, knew from the way she looked at him and touched him, told him that she wanted him.

Her hand was soft, warm against his pounding heart. She looked up at him again, while every werewolf in the room suddenly seemed to tense. The gaze she gave him about melted his soul though.

"What I mean is, if this is your way of saying we're mated," she said, her cheeks once again turning a lovely shade of pink. She took a deep breath. "This is just so different from anything I've ever dreamed of. I need some time…please."

"Our traditions and laws are very old." It was Samantha who spoke, her voice calm and reassuring. "They haven't changed for centuries, and although some of them have needed a bit of work, our laws on mating are honored by all. We understand that they are different for you. And we grant you that time. What my mate wishes for you to know is that when you come to us announcing that mating, it will be approved."

Heather nodded, and thank the moon in the sky, she cuddled into him.

Everyone left after that with little ceremony.

* * * * *

"There is something you will know," he said the moment they were alone.

Heather turned, adoring how the silver sparkled in those deep blue eyes of his. "What's that?"

A charge of energy seemed to rush through him, his body tightening, something about him bordering on dangerous. "When I changed the other day while we were fucking…"

"Yes?" she prompted, running her hands over his large chest while she lowered her gaze. Corded muscles twitched against her touch. Such strength about made her weak in the knees.

"That was intentional—to make you mine."

She hadn't expected him to say that. Her heart seemed to suddenly beat a lot faster, while a tingly warm sensation swam through her.

"But…and you will understand this. Each of us has a soul mate, and we mated because we are meant to be together. However, making it public is what bonds us for life. I would have discussed this with you before announcing it, making it official. Going to my brother, discussing with him what should have been discussed with me, is what brought about this whole ordeal."

Her mouth went dry and she swallowed the lump in her throat. "Sometimes asking a stranger is easier than asking someone you care about."

"True. And because you did that, you brought around the blessing of your being part of this pack possibly a lot faster than if things had been done differently. And you have mated us."

"What you call mating, I consider marriage." She leaned into him, wrapping her arms around his powerful neck, and pulling his face closer to hers. "And, my sexy werewolf, I will let you know if and when I'm ready for that."

Marc straightened, the dangerous look in his eyes growing as silver hues streaked through the blue. He grew before her, muscles stretching against his shirt.

"You are mine, Heather. Call it what you want." His mouth barely moved when he spoke, and although he sounded calm, she knew he meant that they were mated.

"You don't tell me that I'm yours." She had to lean her head back now just to look up at him, but damn it, he wouldn't ever bully her. "You will ask."

"I already know that you want me. And I want you. There is nothing to ask."

"Ask."

Her knees wobbled but she wouldn't take a step backwards. No matter that he was almost twice her size, it would be a cold day in hell when he thought he could manipulate her like this.

Marc stared down at her for a moment. Emotions warred through him. She could tell by the way his body hardened, by the slight twitch at the edge of his mouth. As hard-assed as he was, when they were alone, Heather would never submit to him. Not in any way. And she damn well deserved the courtesy of being asked if she wanted to be his woman.

"Heather." He growled her name, sending chills clear down to her toes. "I need you to be mine."

She knew she was pushing him, that his nature didn't allow any submissiveness on his part. But damn it, she had to know.

"Do you love me?"

The way his eyes widened, the slight twitch that appeared at the side of his mouth, delighted her more than anything he could have said.

"Little bitch," he whispered, his expression brooding. "I've never felt for another bitch the way I feel for you. And yes, I think it might be love."

She couldn't stop from grinning, her bad-ass werewolf had shared his feelings with her, feelings and emotions so easily displayed when he changed into a beast, yet somehow stuffed down further than most humans when he was a man.

"I think I love you too," she whispered. "And yes, if you agree to be mine, then I will be yours. But that's as far as it goes today. No public announcements for a while…please."

"No public announcements," he agreed.

Marc scooped her into his arms, lifting her off the ground as if she weighed next to nothing. She wished she had the strength to rip his clothes off. More than anything she wanted his flesh pressed against hers, the bristle of his chest hairs tickling her skin, the hardness of his body stretched out underneath her.

It had been a hell of a few days, and she ached to fuck him, to initiate the beginning of something more serious between them. When he managed to unzip her dress before placing her on his bed, she hurried to wiggle out of it.

"Naked. I need you naked." Good God, she was almost panting.

Marc chuckled, a sound that sent chills of anticipation rushing through her.

"You stay away from me intentionally, making me suffer without you, and then think you can just have what you want the second you want it?"

"Yup. Sounds damn good to me." She reached for his jeans but he backed away from her.

She didn't understand when he opened a drawer to his dresser and pulled out a few pieces of clothing.

"What's this?" she asked, staring at the flannel shirt he handed her.

"Just a minute, I think there are some old sweats here that might fit you."

"What the hell are you doing?" She knelt on his bed, completely naked, glaring at his backside as he rummaged through several of his drawers before finding what he wanted and holding them toward her. "You want me to put on old baggy clothes?"

"Well, for tonight it's the best that I have for you." The mischievous look he gave her made her want to smack him. He tossed the clothing on the bed next to her. "Put them on. We're going on a run and I don't want you to freeze that cute little ass of yours off."

This wasn't exactly what she'd had in mind. But she had to admit, it was fun putting on his clothes, his musky scent wrapping around her as she drowned in the clothing. Next he found her an old jacket and then led her out to his deck.

Watching him strip in the darkness was so damned erotic. She felt ugly as sin bundled up in his clothing, but could tell how excited he was to take her with him.

"There's no bike here. How do you expect me to keep up with you?"

"You're going to ride me, little bitch."

She would have asked him what he meant by that but Marc began changing. His body contorted, muscles bulging so fiercely underneath his skin she wondered how he managed not to scream in pain.

Without thought, she reached out, knowing her action was ridiculous. Marc worshipped the change, gloried in releasing his raw, untamed energy. This was what made him whole, so much more man than any human.

His cheekbones broadened, while his nose seemed to lower on his face. Bones altered, transforming him. She wondered if she would ever get accustomed to how he altered, morphed with a silence and grace into the giant beast that stood before her just a minute later.

Her heart raced in her chest. Marc was a ferocious looking creature. Large dagger-like teeth pressed against his fur. Larger than any dog, any wolf—hell, possibly larger than a bear, not that she'd ever stood next to one. And those silver eyes, almond-shaped and too wise to belong to any animal, stared at her, blinking slowly. Heather's mouth went dry. This creature was the same being who had stood before her and the man that she loved. The beast before her was simply another part of Marc.

He lowered his head, looking even more deadly, if that were possible, and let out a low growl. When he stepped toward her, rubbing against her, she managed to get her mind to work.

"You want me to ride you?"

That's what he'd said. She ran her hands through his thick white coat, and then held on while she climbed onto his back. Then she held on for dear life as he started off with a slow pace through the backyard.

It took a few minutes, and Marc didn't rush in picking up his pace, but Heather managed to get comfortable, leaning forward and resting her chest against his back. Solid muscle twitched against her with a steady rhythm as he began running, taking them into open countryside.

Her man—her werewolf—was sharing the other half of who he was with her. And her heart swelled as she relaxed, and ran her hands over his rough coat.

"I love you, Marc McAllister," she whispered into his ear, and she swore he looked like he was laughing.

Enjoy an excerpt from:
PURSUIT

Thoughts of the night her sire had gone to that blasted pack meeting, informing her that he would announce her dowry, find her a mate, made her stomach turn.

"I don't need help finding a mate," she'd argued with him.

"You'll do as you're told. I won't have a werewolf shacking up alongside me that I don't approve of."

"But I'll have to live with him."

Her sire had thrown his arms up in the air, turning to glare at her mother, and then had stormed out. It had been later that night that Jordan Ricky, drunk as a skunk from celebrating his mating to her, had found her. The *Cariboo* in her pack had confirmed and celebrated her mating without even talking to her about it. How fucking barbaric could a pack be.

Pamela rested her head on her knees, refusing to feel sorry for herself. That would get her nowhere. *Take action. Don't wallow in pity.* Her mother's soft-spoken words still encouraged her forward.

It was time once again to take action. Jordan Ricky was here. This was a larger pack, with what she hoped was more forward thinking than her own pack. There was no doubt in her head though that the pack leader here would honor the words of her own pack leader. They all seemed to think they had to control their bitches. Like she didn't have a mind of her own.

The ache to lunge through the window, spring to the ground below and race across the bountiful land outside sounded so damn good.

She stayed put though, sitting on her bed in the small bedroom she'd considered sanctuary. Waiting quietly until the house grew quiet, as the day began, she didn't move until she knew she could escape without being noticed.

Simone left the house with the cubs, taking them to school, and that was the moment Pamela waited for. Once the bitch of the den was gone, she had a better chance of escape. The werewolves wouldn't pay as much attention to her. Werewolf culture was the same no matter the pack or breeding. The bitches answered to the bitches. It was the way it was in this den, and the way it had always been.

Running in her fur during the day was a dangerous and more than likely foolish feat. Accepting the fact that she would have to hoof it across the meadows toward the miles of rambling trees that surrounded the lumberyard where Gabe worked, she put speed to her gait, running faster than a human could run.

Maybe running to Gabe wasn't the answer. She knew little about this *Cariboo*. For all she knew, he might be as bad as Jordan.

No fucking way! Quit being paranoid. No Cariboo could be as bad as Jordan.

The chilly air didn't stop her from breaking out in a sweat. By the time the rich smell of freshly cut wood filled her senses, her heart pounded in her chest, partially from running so fast, and more so from the excitement of seeing Gabe again.

And what if he wants nothing to do with you?

Remembering when they were last together, his hands on her, his mouth nipping at her neck, made her heart race all the faster. She could barely keep her breath when she heard pounding footsteps racing behind her. Turning quickly, ready to take on her pursuer, she didn't have time to react when a large body slammed into her, taking her to the ground.

"Where the hell do you think you're going?" Gabe's growl ripped through her.

Panic had consumed her. Too many memories of Jordan tracking her down, capturing her every time she'd tried to escape his mountain cabin, rushed through her before she realized who was on top of her.

Kicking furiously, she bit and scratched while Gabe lifted her to her feet.

"Calm down, my sweet bitch." His tone was relaxed, not the nasty criticism she'd heard so many times from Jordan.

It took a moment to catch her breath. Gabe put her on her feet, running his hands down her arms before releasing her. He put his hands on his hips, staring down at her, looking at her as if he waited for an explanation.

"Jordan. Jordan Ricky." She inhaled deeply, ordering her heart to quit pounding in her chest. "He's here. He's in Prince George."

"And so you run from your protection? Are you trying to seek him out?" Gabe didn't look pleased.

His aggravation filled the air around them. Anger filled her nose with its spicy aroma. Pamela nibbled her lower lip, forcing herself to remain calm at his preposterous implication. Were all werewolves so damned bull-headed?

"Hell no, I don't want to seek him out." She matched his stance, fisting her hands against her hips. "I overheard them this morning. They are worried about Jordan bringing his pack to the ranch. I'm going to bring trouble to them and I won't have that."

"And so where are you going?"

"I was looking for you."

Something changed in his expression. Gabe grew before her, his muscles bulging while his mouth formed a thin, determined line.

There was no way she could move when he reached for her, grabbing her tangled hair and pulling it to the side, forcing her to arch backwards as he tugged.

"You won't turn me away twice," he grumbled, and then captured her mouth with fiery need.

So many emotions had tumbled through her since she'd awoken that morning. The exhilaration of her run, even if while in her skin, had unleashed adrenaline that now needed a direction. Without thinking, she reached for Gabe, gripping his hair as he did hers, and holding on, deepening the kiss.

When he growled into her mouth she about exploded inside, moisture soaking her inner thighs against her jeans.

It hadn't crossed her mind what she would do once she found Gabe. But his aggression put all of her energy into focus. More than anything right now she needed to fuck him. Damn the possibility that more of the crewmen could be out here working. She needed him inside her, and she needed him now.

Grabbing his shirt, she ripped at it with her fingernails, hardly giving thought to the partial change rushing through her.

"Woman." His growl fed her fire, the one word giving her chills.

"I'm not turning you away." She could barely talk, barely think.

Ever since overhearing the conversation that morning, knowing Jordan was so close, she'd been in a state of panic. Somehow being in Gabe's arms, feeling his hard body pressed against hers, gave her a sense of grounding.

This *Cariboo* would protect her. She didn't know why she knew that. But instinct told her that he wouldn't hurt her, wouldn't use her like Jordan did. His strong scent, dominating and predatory, wrapped around her. Her pussy throbbed with a demanding need. And more than anything she needed him inside her, realizing that it would bond them, but at the moment not caring.

Gabe's hand moved between them, grabbing onto the waist of her jeans. With a quick tug he ripped the button free...

Why an electronic book?

 We live in the Information Age — an exciting time in the history of human civilization, in which technology rules supreme and continues to progress in leaps and bounds every minute of every day. For a multitude of reasons, more and more avid literary fans are opting to purchase e-books instead of paper books. The question from those not yet initiated into the world of electronic reading is simply: *Why?*

1. ***Price.*** An electronic title at Ellora's Cave Publishing and Cerridwen Press runs anywhere from 40% to 75% less than the cover price of the exact same title in paperback format. Why? Basic mathematics and cost. It is less expensive to publish an e-book (no paper and printing, no warehousing and shipping) than it is to publish a paperback, so the savings are passed along to the consumer.

2. ***Space.*** Running out of room in your house for your books? That is one worry you will never have with electronic books. For a low one-time cost, you can purchase a handheld device specifically designed for e-reading. Many e-readers have large, convenient screens for viewing. Better yet, hundreds of titles can be stored within your new library — on a single microchip. There are a variety of e-readers from different manufacturers. You can also read e-books on your PC or laptop computer. (Please note that Ellora's Cave does not endorse any specific brands.

You can check our websites at www.ellorascave.com or www.cerridwenpress.com for information we make available to new consumers.)

3. *Mobility.* Because your new e-library consists of only a microchip within a small, easily transportable e-reader, your entire cache of books can be taken with you wherever you go.

4. *Personal Viewing Preferences.* Are the words you are currently reading too small? Too large? Too... ANNOYING? Paperback books cannot be modified according to personal preferences, but e-books can.

5. *Instant Gratification.* Is it the middle of the night and all the bookstores near you are closed? Are you tired of waiting days, sometimes weeks, for bookstores to ship the novels you bought? Ellora's Cave Publishing sells instantaneous downloads twenty-four hours a day, seven days a week, every day of the year. Our webstore is never closed. Our e-book delivery system is 100% automated, meaning your order is filled as soon as you pay for it.

Those are a few of the top reasons why electronic books are replacing paperbacks for many avid readers.

As always, Ellora's Cave and Cerridwen Press welcome your questions and comments. We invite you to email us at Comments@ellorascave.com or write to us directly at Ellora's Cave Publishing Inc., 1056 Home Avenue, Akron, OH 44310-3502.

erridwen, the Celtic Goddess of wisdom, was the muse who brought inspiration to storytellers and those in the creative arts. Cerridwen Press encompasses the best and most innovative stories in all genres of today's fiction. Visit our site and discover the newest titles by talented authors who still get inspired - much like the ancient storytellers did, once upon a time.

Cerridwen Press

www.cerridwenpress.com

Discover for yourself why readers can't get enough
of the multiple award-winning publisher
Ellora's Cave.

Whether you prefer e-books or paperbacks,

be sure to visit EC on the web at
www.ellorascave.com

for an erotic reading experience that will leave you
breathless.